GIRL OUT OF WATER

GiRL OUT OF WATER

NAT LUURTSEMA

WALKER
BOOKS

First published 2016 by Walker Books Ltd
87 Vauxhall Walk, London SE11 5HJ

4 6 8 10 9 7 5 3

Text © 2016 Nat Luurtsema
Cover images: goggles © 2016 LWA/Larry Williams/Getty Images;
hair © 2016 moodboard/Getty Images;
face © 2016 Hill Street Studios/Getty Images

This book has been typeset in Sabon

Printed and bound in Great Britain by Clays Ltd, St Ives plc

British Library Cataloguing in Publication Data:
a catalogue record for this book is available from the British Library

ISBN 978-1-4063-6652-5

www.walker.co.uk

For Diarmuid

PROLOGUE

You'd think it would feel weird being nearly naked in front of so many people, but it doesn't.

I ping my swimsuit straps for luck, once right, twice left, walk out poolside and take a deep breath, inhaling the familiar tang of chlorine and feet. It sounds gross, but that smell is so exciting: I'm where I belong.

I'm one of the fastest swimmers in my county. That's why I'm here – trying out for High Performance Training Camp, which will set me on my way to Team GB. I've wanted this for as long as I can remember. So ... you know, no pressure, not a big deal, whatev.

I think I'm sweating inside my ears.

I pad along the side of the pool watching other swimmers power up and down; they look so strong, they're not so much swimming as punching their way through the water.

We're all in a vast... I want to use the word palace. I'm going to. It's a palace made of glass, filled with four Olympic-sized swimming pools. Basically my dream home. The sound of splashing and shouting bounces off the walls. Ninety per cent of the people in this room are having the most important day of their lives.

I look around for my best friend, Hannah, and spot her by the changing rooms. I give her a quick smile. She does an elaborate mime of puking into the pool. Feeling a bit queasy, then. An official eyes her disapprovingly.

I tuck a stray hair into my swimming cap with a shaking hand.

Hannah rotates her shoulders backwards and then forwards. She swims butterfly, which gives you really big shoulders, but she's not self-conscious about it – she just wears men's T-shirts. People love Hannah. She's fun. She has thick, blonde curly hair and big blue eyes and she never stops talking. She's been my best friend since we were six, and now, looking at how nervous she is, I find myself feeling protective even though I'm in the same position.

Well, not exactly the same: her parents are really

pushy. She tries to ignore it or it would drive her mad. Mine reckon swimming is less important than – well, LOADS of stuff.

Hannah's standing next to me now. She grins and pulls at the front of my swimming cap. I fold my arms and pretend to ignore her. She pulls the elastic six inches away from my forehead and I brace myself for her to snap it, but instead she nudges her face next to mine and starts trying to pull my swimming cap over her head as well as mine. Ridiculous human being. This is why I bring spare caps.

I can't keep a straight face. I start giggling and help her pull the thick elastic further over her head. It hurts – her nose is digging hard into my cheekbone – but I'm determined to get it on. *Beep!* Hannah's eyes widen at the sound of the whistle. This is her race!

She hurriedly pulls her head away, causing her own swimming cap to ping off and nearly land in the nearest pool. I can see a couple of officials looking at us, unimpressed. *Sor-ree.* Just trying to lighten a very heavy mood here. I dive to retrieve Hannah's cap while she fights her frizzy mop into a bun.

We hug quickly and she hurries to the pool where the butterfly swimmers are waiting by the diving blocks.

Some serious shoulders amongst that lot.

Now I'm alone and back to feeling sick about my own race. I tuck my ears into my swimming cap and everything becomes a smooth roar. An official comes to check my name against a list on her clipboard. I can't help but notice that she has a very fluffy top lip. She catches me staring at it and I quickly look down.

"Louise?" she asks.

"Brown," I say to her shoe, and she ticks my name off.

She must be one of only ten people in the whole place who aren't feeling hysterical. If the fire alarm went off, I swear we'd all run around in circles, screaming and slapping our own faces.

My race is called next and I join a line of girls who look just like me. Tall girls with no hips, no boobs and frizzy hair are the norm here. I'm going to fit in so well in the training camp! Finally, someone to borrow clothes off.

I look around for Hannah's and my coach, Debs. She's standing by the pool where I'll be doing my race, arms folded, staring intently at me. She gives me a nod. She's not the most affectionate person: that nod means, "Go on, Lou, I know you can do it! Supportive things, etc!"

Up on the blocks I scuff my feet and stare dead ahead. You swim no one's race but your own.

The official nods and I bend into my dive, wrapping my fingertips over the edge of the block and swaying gently to loosen my hips. There's a pause that feels never ending and I focus on the spot in the water where I want my dive to take me.

The starting pistol bangs, there's an explosion of power from my legs and I dive hard. I can hear the block rattle as I push away from it with all my strength. A cold, hard slap against my thighs and I spring into butterfly stroke. Hannah's faster at this, but I'm pretty good too. I whip my arms up and over my head. My fingers cut into the water in front of my face. As my arms pull down, my hips tilt and my legs kick together like a mermaid's tail. This is the closest I ever get to elegant.

Backstroke now, my second fastest stroke, and I hold my head steady as I stare up at the ceiling. I practised this last night when everyone else had finished training. I count signposts on the ceiling so I don't ram my head into the side of the pool and slow myself down. Debs says this is the mindset of a consummate pro.

I had to google consummate. It's either a compliment or a French soup.

I feel so happy when I swim, strong and graceful and like everything is right with the world. This is my Thing.

The individual medley is a strange race. Most people are slowest on their breaststroke, fastest on the crawl. I'm the other way around, so I always pull ahead on laps five and six, hopefully opening up enough of a lead that some freakish monkey-armed girl with a devastating crawl time can't catch me on seven and eight.

And here's seven and eight – harder when everyone's so powerful; the water is churning and throwing me about. So much for feeling graceful, this is like fighting water. But I can't sense anyone on the left or right of me. I must have pulled ahead. Excellent: it's all going to plan.

Now it's about hanging on to this lead. I carve my right hand back past my face to make a groove in the water just long enough to turn my head and grab a huge, ragged breath. It's difficult in this choppy water so each time I'm just praying I find air. I can't afford to choke.

Final lap and now I'm completely in my rhythm, I know the end is approaching but I have to keep swimming my hardest so no one catches me. I don't care if I smash my head into the edge of the pool – anything to maintain this speed to the end. My wrist hits something hard with a crack that I feel down to my hip, but I've done it.

I've done it! I've won.

I fling my head out of the water, rip off my swimming cap and goggles, squeeze the water from my eyes and look behind me. That's my first thought: how far behind are they?

But there's no one there.

They're all next to me. Everyone. There is *no one* behind me, no one still swimming.

The girl on my left looks bored, the one on the right is casually cleaning her goggles with spit. Oh my... *One of them is already out of the pool!* I did that once, against a rubbish team in Swindon that was so slow I got out before the last girl had finished. Debs had a go at me for that. Unsportspersonlike, she said.

Debs! Where is she, where's my coach? Maybe I swam extra lengths by mistake? That must be it. Hilarious, of course that's what happened. Dumb but understandable on a high-pressure day. This is not a Big Deal. Shall I talk to someone, an official? Where is everyone going? Coach! Debs! Hello? No one is looking me in the eye. Did I *die* in that pool, am I a ghost?

I might as well be. I came last. For the first time since

I started competing at ten years old, I was the slowest swimmer. I'm weak and cold, my legs heavy as the adrenalin drops out of me. I don't know what to do, where to go...

I have to find Hannah. I look around frantically for her. There she is! She's throwing back her hair, laughing and shaking hands with an official, who's handing her a slip of paper. She must have won her race. She catches my eye and her smile fades.

My best friend and I want to kill her.

1

My pillow smells. I should've changed the pillowcase weeks ago but I haven't and now it smells of my head. Which I did not realize was so smelly.

I can hear my family moving around downstairs, slamming drawers and clattering bowls. I'm not used to these morning noises because I'd usually be up at 5 a.m. and training by 6 a.m. Forty lengths of breaststroke, forty backstroke, forty crawl, ten butterfly, then a quick shower, sleepwalk through school and back in the pool by 4 p.m. YOLO!

But I haven't swum since the time trials three weeks ago and now I'm stuck with a surprising number of useless hours. Who knew days were so long? I sometimes used to wonder what I was missing as I pounded out the lengths in the pool. Now I know: NOTHING.

Except I'd never met our postman before, and he has a lot of nose hair. That's it.

My name's Lou and I am a fifteen-year-old ex-swimmer. I have an older sister, Lavender. Yup, Lou and Lav. We have a brother called Toilet.

That's a lie. It's just me, Lav, Mum and Dad, in a small semi-detached house in the most boring town in the world.

So this summer I stopped swimming and met our postman. And finally got all that crying done that I'd been meaning to do for ages, so that's good, isn't it? Plus I really explored the concept of Lying in Bed All Day Feeling Nothing But Despair. A summer lived right to the edges.

It's the first day of school today. I'd mark the occasion by wearing a dress, but I don't own one. In our most private moments, Hannah and I have accepted that the only way we'll find a dress to fit our shoulders is if we go to that cross-dressing shop in town. They've got nice stuff in the window. (We'll cut the labels out.)

It's also my first day without Hannah, as she's already left for High Performance Training Camp. Mum says that now we're separated for a bit I'll come out of Hannah's shadow, but she doesn't understand. I liked it there!

Going back to school would be fine if Hannah hadn't got through the time trials either. We could face it together, maybe hint that the competition was a big conspiracy. That we were *too* fast; we'd have threatened international relations at the next Olympics when we smashed everyone out of the water with our awesome times.

"Yeah, well, Russia," we'd have said, with careful looks around us. "They do *not* like silver, if you know what I'm saying." Then we'd have tugged our fedoras down and skulked off to double maths.

Wonder if the other side of my pillow is less smelly? I flip it. Nope.

But now Hannah has gone to the camp without me and I won't see her all term. We're so far away from each other! She's in Dorset and I'm in Essex. She's heading to the Olympics and I'm heading to the bathroom.

Miraculously, it's free – pretty impressive in a house of four people, three of whom take showers you could time with a calendar.

I'm still using that special harsh shampoo for swimmers, the stuff that strips the chlorine out of your hair.

Money is a bit tight at the moment so I have to use it all up first, and we seem to have found a never-ending bottle. I soap my head and reflect that it really doesn't help that the smell reminds me of my old life.

I step out of the shower, fold a towel dress around me (the only kind I fit cos it's sleeveless) and scuff my feet along the hallway. The carpet is a bit worn in patches, so I'm careful not to catch my toe in a snagged thread. No one needs to start their day hopping and screaming.

I open my clothes drawer and drag out some jeans and a T-shirt. I don't have any "nice" clothes. Ever since I was eleven I've been caught up in some desperate, endless growth spurt. There's no point buying decent clothes because they probably won't fit in a month's time. I'm 5'11" and *still* growing.

It's fine: if I ever get a boyfriend I can carry him when he's tired.

I stab a wide-toothed comb gently into my hair because I haven't got time to cut knots out. My hair doesn't grow down, it grows *out*, like Hannah's.

Neither of us looks like the princess in a fairy tale, we look like the enchanted vines that covered her castle for a hundred years.

It was always comforting to have a best friend who

looked as different as me. And we never minded because we had swimming; we had a Thing. Now my Thing is gone and so is my friend.

I can't delay this much longer. I'm going to have to eat some breakfast and then ... gah ... SCHOOL. I swing around the end of the banister and can't help smiling when I catch sight of my family.

The kitchen is too small for the four of us – we only fit in there if everyone stays very still. If you actually want to move, elbows will get jogged and cereal will get tipped down backs. You know your house is cramped when you can start making a sandwich and end up in a food fight.

Dad is cooking (carefully), Mum's reading a book and Lavender is trowelling make-up on to her ridiculously beautiful face. They look like they're in an advert. They don't need a Thing – everyone's just grateful they get to look at them.

I'm proud of them but wish I didn't look adopted.

Mum is half-Indonesian, all curves, shiny hair and smooth, brown skin, while Dad looks like a doctor on an American TV show. Good chin, nice teeth. Admittedly he has a bit of a belly these days, but he just holds his breath for photos. Lavender is sixteen, with glossy black hair, proper boobs and a tattoo that Mum and Dad don't know about.

Nature made her and then, a year later, took the same ingredients and made me. It's baffling. Good thing they didn't have a third child: it would probably have a face like a knee.

"Morning..." I sigh at the room, and they mumble back sleepily. Dad slides a brick of scrambled egg onto my plate as I sit down, while Mum subtly slides Lav's make-up bag away from her.

"Enough, Lavender."

"A little more highlighter and blush and I'm *done*, I swear."

Mum keeps reading as she drops the make-up bag into a drawer next to her. Lav looks mutinous, but she's still got her mascara wand, so she makes good use of it before Mum can reunite it with the bottle.

The mood in the kitchen is a little ... well ... moody. Lav's grounded because she was caught sneaking out late at night with a bottle of Malibu. She swears she wasn't going to drink it, but what else – walk it? As Mum said, if she's taking bottles of rum for midnight walks, she should be kept indoors for her own safety.

I poke up a forkful of egg and stare at it. Eyes down,

I say, "Um. Caaaan *I*…"

"No," Mum says.

"You don't even know what I was going to say!"

Mum imitates my voice with annoying accuracy. "Can I not go to school today or maybe ever, can I just get a job instead, and we'll lie and tell everyone at school that I changed my name, had plastic surgery and made it into Team GB after all?"

Damn. Spot on.

Lavender finishes applying her thirty-second coat of mascara and leans towards me as if she's going to impart the secret of immortality.

Expectations low, I lean towards her.

"It's going to be OK at school," she says.

"Really?"

"Yes. Because no one cares about your swimming. Only you think it's a big deal."

"It *is* a big deal!"

"Shut up, I'm trying to help you. I swear, if anyone even *mentions* swimming – which they won't – and you tell them what happened, they'll say, 'Huh.' And they won't ever think of it again. It's boring. No one cares. Amelia Bond from 12K? She had her big hairy face mole removed over the summer. *That* is interesting."

I'm unconvinced but not willing to have an argument about it. She's wrong; it's not true that no one cares. Hannah cares. Hannah understands that swimming is extremely important. But thinking about Hannah feels like poking a blister, so I make myself stop.

Dad slings the saucepan into the sink. He does all the cooking: Mum's speciality dish is food poisoning.

"You girls ready to leave for school in ten?"

"Shotgun!"

"Lav! You always sit in the front!"

"Yes. Because I always call shotgun. Please stop me if this confuses you."

"Fine. Infinity shotgun!"

"You can't call infinity shotgun, everyone knows that," says Mum. "Now off you go."

"Are you home tonight, Mum?" I ask.

"Uh, no, I have a—"

"Daa-aate!" we all chorus.

"So go on," Lav says, "what's his name?"

Mum hesitates.

"It's OK, Flora," says Dad, kindly. "If you don't know it, you don't have to pretend."

"You could check his wallet when he goes to the toilet?" Lav suggests.

"Though if he takes it with him he's possibly not coming back," I add.

Mum gives out three death stares and returns to her book.

Yeah, date. It's a bit odd in this house.

Mum and Dad divorced when I was little but are the nicest divorced couple. They never fight and they get on really well. I'm not sure why they divorced, but I don't want to ask in case the answer involves sex and I *never* stop being sick.

Dad lost his job last year and he's had to move in with us until he finds a new one. It's taking a lot longer than he thought it would. Sometimes when he leaves his email open I see all the rejections in his inbox.

It's not ideal, Lav and I having to share a room, but we don't say anything because we don't want to hurt his feelings. I worry about him. He gets up early every morning like he's still got a job and dresses in a suit and then just … I don't know … waits for the day to pass until we come home.

It's like having a smartly dressed but depressed dog.

Between me and him, this house hasn't been much fun this summer. No wonder Lav is taking bottles for walks and Mum is dating like the men are off to war.

It's awkward, actually, as Mum is really enjoying her job, she teaches creative writing to grown-ups. Which sounds like an easy job to me, but she says I haven't read enough bad sexy poetry to judge. (And no, she won't let me see it.)

We call goodbye to Mum and trudge out to the car. Lav forces me into the back, which is not easy. Three-door cars are such a lie – you can't call it three doors unless you see the boot as an acceptable way to get in.

Lavender fiddles with the radio until she finds a pirate station. It sounds like people shouting in a cramped space. As if she doesn't get enough of that at home.

"Oh, Lav, you're so alternative. I cannot get my head around how non-mainstream you are," I sigh, from behind my knees. "Move your seat forward."

Lav squeezes the lever and slowly pushes her seat back as far as it goes, crushing me into an even tighter S shape.

"It's garage, divvy."

"Is that the name of the music or just *where* they are? Come on, Lav, seat forward!"

"*Lavender!*" says Dad. "Move the seat forward or you can walk the rest of the way. Do you want to walk in those shoes? *Can* you walk in those shoes?"

I peer round to see what Dad's talking about. Lav is wearing studded black chunky boots. It looks like she's got weapons on her feet.

"Yes, I can! Not very far, or fast, or..."

"I don't know why you do that to your feet," Dad sighs.

"You don't get me, Mark," she sighs back dramatically.

"*Dad*," he corrects her.

"No, Lav, *everyone* gets you," I say, defending him. "You're so instantly gettable that if you were an exam question everyone would be happy to see you. And that's the only time they'd be happy to— Ow! Legs, legs, legs!"

As Dad approaches the school gates I can see a tall boy with long hair, loitering. Lav slumps down in her seat.

"Drive, drive, drive!" she hisses.

"What?" Dad asks, but he continues past the school gates.

"Uh..."

"Was that Beau Michaels waiting for you?" I ask.

"Yes, and shut up. Dad, can you drop us at the back entrance, please?"

"Wait." Dad is puzzled. "Someone called their son *Beau* and that was allowed to happen?"

"Daa-aad!" Lav rolls her eyes.

"Like, no one was arrested? They were just allowed to do that to an innocent child?" he asks.

"You're not funny," Lav tells him firmly.

Dad circles a mini-roundabout and heads back to the main school entrance.

"No, no, no!" Lav slumps down in her seat again. "I mean, you're hilarious, Dad! Properly witty!"

"I think so," he agrees serenely, and we sail past the entrance again, poor Beau Michaels watching us with the dawning realization that all is not well in his love life.

Dad pulls up at the back entrance to school. Lav hops out and flips her seat forward and I unfold myself into a normal shape. Well, normal for me.

"Come on, LouLou," says Dad.

I pick at some dry skin on my lip and avoid his gaze. Maybe Dad will get bored of waiting and just let me sit quietly in the back of the car for a few years. Eventually I'll be old enough to shuffle forward and share the driving.

Lav leans down at my window.

"I *swear*," she says, "this isn't a big deal unless you make it a big deal. You *nearly* got to the Olympics. That's the closest anyone I know in this crappy little town has ever got to achieving anything! No offence, Dad."

("No, that's fine.")

"So, please, just don't even *mention* it. Now the school day begins and you do not know me."

She wobbles away on her monstrous shoes. She looks like a gazelle, I can't imagine how daft I look when I clump along behind her. The gazelle and the mammoth, off on their adventures.

That thought makes me even sadder, so I push it aside and give Dad a brave smile. My dry lip splits and bleeds.

"It's going to be a good day," he promises.

"OK," I mumble through blood and the semi-clean tissue I find in the door handle. I clamber out of the car and follow Lav at the agreed distance of six feet.

2

Weez!! I can't believe I've been here a week. Time's flying! People are nice but I haven't scoped out any proper friends yet. (You have no grounds for jel.) I'm learning so much. I thought everyone would be terrifyingly good, but I'm OK, you know? Not saying I'm the best but I think I've got a chance. I MISS YOU.

    Hxxxxxx

Lav and I don't hang out at school – she's in the year above, and we're so different, I'm not sure people know we're related. She's popular but seems to get in endless rows with other girls. She reckons they're intimidated by her maturity.

I think it's because she gets off with their boyfriends.

I used to head into school with Hannah, exhausted

and damp from swimming, do a bit of work, have a couple of chats with people (well, she would, I'd hang out in her shadow – *happily*, thanks Mum) then head back to the pool. Hannah and I always treated school like a chore, like the Queen snipping a ribbon on a hospital wing.

I don't think we missed much; our school is very ordinary. A horse walked into the playing field six years ago and people *still* talk about it.

But despite my whingeing, I have resolved to make an effort. Today I'm launching Operation: Make Friends. I'm an idiot for only having one friend. I need a spare!

I'm so used to having Hannah's arm slung around me as we laugh at nine years' worth of stupid private jokes. I've got all my halves of those jokes and nothing to do with them.

I feel a bit shy as I enter my form room, so I check my bag to make me look busy, not lonely. Classic move. I look through my books and pencils. Yup, all there. Hi, guys.

I get so carried away with my acting that I trip over, my rucksack swings around with surprising force and eight small objects fall out. What eight small objects? you ask.

Eight tampons.

ARGH!

What is *wrong* with tampons? Seems like every time I open my bag they leap out in a group suicide bid. I haven't even started my period yet, they're just in case. My face burning, I crouch and start shovelling them back into my bag, desperate for this moment to end. It couldn't get worse.

Yes, it could. I feel a light tap on my head – someone is "helping" by throwing an escaped tampon at me.

And then Mr Peters races in late. Brilliant. The nicest teacher in school (and not bad looking, actually, if you like cardigans) begins his morning by falling over me as I scrabble around on the floor, chasing tampons and trying not to cry.

The class falls silent as he comes over and helps me to my feet. I like Mr Peters, he's one of the few people in school taller than me – and not in a stooped, have-to-get-my-shoes-specially-made-in-America sort of way.

I give him a "thank you and that never happened" smile and weave through to our desk at the back. *My* desk now. Teachers always knew they could sit Hannah and me there. We weren't particularly *good* students, but we were quiet. You don't need to pass notes to someone you've known that long.

I sit down, face still hot, and hope everyone develops amnesia by lunch. I don't want to be Tampon Brown all term.

"Did you see that video I posted on your wall?" one of the two boys in front of me says to his friend, and I lean forward to join in. After a bad start, Operation: Make Friends begins *right now*.

"Yeah! That guy looked so much like Hatsy it blew my mind."

"That's why I put it up there!"

"Oh, right! But everyone looks like Hatsy."

They collapse into quiet hysterics for some reason.

I'm watching the conversation go back and forth, feeling the smile die on my face.

Who is Hatsy? Is it funny that everyone looks like him? Apparently. And what was that video? This conversation is like code. There's no way I can join in.

"Double chemistry next, nightmare!" I say to the back of their heads in a matey, eye-rolly sort of way. But too quietly, so they don't realize I'm talking to them. I look out of the window and bite my nail. I'm not embarrassed, I'm busy! Busy biting this nail.

"Sorry, did you say something?" One of the boys turns around.

I nod, suddenly choking on a piece of nail. Now I'm coughing right in his face. *Right in his face.*

"No talking at the back!" Mr Peters calls over. The boys turn back, one of them frowning and wiping his face.

I sit, stunned by my own social idiocy, and wonder if I will ever stop blushing or if my family could use my head as a radiator and cut their heating bills.

Then I'd have to be home-schooled, right?

My phone vibrates up my sleeve and I slide it out for a peek. It's a text from Mum, a picture of a badly stuffed otter. She may be grumpy in the mornings (and some afternoons and evenings) but she gets me – bad taxidermy always makes me laugh.

There's a photo of an annoyed-looking stuffed fox holding a handbag that never stops being funny, no matter how many times I look at it (and I needed to look at that fox *a lot* this summer). I scroll around my phone and then tap my inbox.

I really should reply to Hannah's last message. We've been chatting every day, but she starts all the conversations and I feel like everything I write is fake – things like: I'm sooooooo happy for yoooooo! Xxxxx.

I'm a very bad liar.

After the time trials, I did my best to seem OK, although I sat at the front of the minibus instead of at the back with Hannah because I suddenly developed carsickness.

I kept staring up at the ceiling because the fake carsickness was also making my eyes water. "Anyone else got wet eyes? I think it's the air-conditioning. Look, my eyes are so wet they're actually *leaking*!" (Sniff.)

Hannah had always been good, but I never realized she was so much better than me. I think she swam one of her fastest times ever that day. I don't know my time; officials don't chase after the girls who come last.

Hannah was so excited and I didn't want to spoil it. That night I texted her loads, things like: I'm so proud of you my fish!!! Xxxxxxx.

Which is a bit fake and gushy, but You stole my dreams!! is not a cool thing to text your best friend, even if it's true.

And I *am* happy for her! I'm just sad for me.

"Louise?" I look up, Mr Peters is staring and people are starting to turn and roll their eyes. What have I done *now*?

"Yee-urp?" I say stupidly, and he smiles at me, a little exasperated, and says, "Sasha Burrows?"

Oh. The register. Right.

The morning begins with history, where I learn a lot of really cool things, like how I KNOW NOTHING ABOUT HISTORY AND I AM BASICALLY AS EDU-CATED AS A PIECE OF TOAST.

See, *this* is the problem with planning to be a pro-fessional swimmer for the rest of your life; you don't think that you might need an education. Basically, the moment I could read I felt educated enough. After that, I used school time to relax in. Can't believe I hadn't noticed how behind I'd got. Clearly me and Han were oblivious in our bubble of idiot.

My history teacher corners me after class to say, "How exciting about Hannah, you must be so proud!"

"Yes, yes, I am, I really am!" I say back at her, nod-ding hard with big, fake eyes.

History is followed by chemistry, because this school believes in putting the boring in edu-boring-cation.

It's amazing how little I know in this subject too. I listen hard and take lots of notes. Maybe I'm an academic genius; perhaps *that's* my actual Thing, not swimming after all.

"Any ideas? Anyone?"

I shoot my hand in the air.

"Louise!"

"Potassium!"

"No. Pota… What? I haven't mentioned potassium once this lesson."

"Oh, OK."

People snigger. The teacher stares at me, baffled. "Did you mean *phosphorus*?"

"Uh. Yeah?"

"That's still wrong."

Finally the morning's over and it's lunch. I follow the smell of cabbage until I'm at the canteen. (We hardly ever have cabbage, there's just this lingering smell. Mysterious.)

I look around. I knew this would happen: there's no one to sit with and every table "belongs" to a friendship group, so I wouldn't just be eating there, I'd look like I was trying to join their group. I don't want to be ignored – or, worse, told to get lost.

Can I bring my own little table into school every day?

I buy a sandwich, stick it in my rucksack and head outside, daydreaming about my new (unlikely) future as a chemistry genius. My first breakthrough would be to disprove its credibility as a subject, forcing thousands of unemployed chemistry teachers to rethink their snotty attitudes.

I walk in a circle around school, eating my sandwich. It's boring having no one to talk to. I take out my phone. I'm tempted to call Hannah, but then we'd have to talk about training camp and the thought of *that* makes my food stick in my throat.

As I'm choking and spluttering, eyes watering, phone in hand, Mr Peters appears next to me. He raises his eyebrows at the phone, which I'm not allowed to have out during the school day. I wave it weakly and whisper, "Ambulance."

He gives a snort of laughter and keeps walking.

He stops and turns back.

"Lou, you *are* joking?"

I nod, putting my phone away. He makes a *phew!* gesture and keeps walking.

Great, I've found someone I can chat to – and they're paid to talk to me.

As I'm putting my phone back in my bag, I realize I've stopped in front of the one place that can help me.

The library.

Home of the introverted and people too quiet to say, "No, Lou, I don't want to be your friend. Leave me alone to read. Get that friendship bracelet *off* me. No, *you* shush!"

3

I settle down in one of the booths and feel myself relaxing for the first time all day. I quietly finish the last of my sandwich, eyes darting about for the librarian. She's a small, nervy, hissing woman, and if that makes her sound like a terrifying animal, then *good*.

I'm in the Sports section. It's only about a shelf long, but there's a tattered old book there called *Swimming for Women and the Infirm*. Brilliant! I pull it down and start reading. It smells musty and is adorably nuts, focusing on "making elegant, ladylike shapes" rather than actually going anywhere. I'd love to see the look on Debs' face if I tried this. "Personal best? No, I'm making a star shape, wheee!"

I haven't seen Debs in weeks. After the time trials she suggested I "take a break" from swimming, which was a pretty unsubtle dumping. Last year my team trained before school, after school, sometimes at lunchtimes and weekends, and we'd all been working towards these time trials. Now I'd flunked, there didn't seem to be much point in carrying on. I'd just get in everyone's way, being slow, crying, trailing ribbons of snot behind me... I thought of asking for another chance. I could always try out next year, but what if I came last *again*?

I tell Hannah this on our last sleepover of the summer. It's still warm out, so we're camping – our last chance before she's off to Dorset. As I babble on about my worries, she looks uncomfortable. She's my best friend, of course she's not going to say, "Yeah, train for another year! I'm sure you won't choke again!" but she can't say, "Give up, pal, you're clearly rubbish," either.

We sit, chewing in silence. I'm eating cereal out of the packet and Hannah's eating a block of concentrated jelly, which is disgusting, but she reckons it stops her nails splitting from all the chlorine in the pool. Plus side, she always smells fruity.

Thankfully for her, she's saved from giving me careers advice.

"SLUG!"

There's a huge one shuffling its disgusting belly up

the inside of our tent. Our screams bring Hannah's mum down to the bottom of the garden. (Because yes, of course we're camping in the back garden; we're not heroes.)

Barbra's just got in from a shift at the hospital and she isn't in the best of moods. When you work in A&E, two girls shrieking over a slug can seem a bit small-fry. She flicks it mercilessly into the hedge, ignoring our pleas to (a) be gentle, and (b) escort it to a leaf ten or twenty miles away, please.

Babs (as I have *never* dared call her) then pops her head back into the tent and stares at me for a moment with a concerned look on her face.

"Lou, have you *done something* to your hair?"

She looks horrified. Classic Babs. She's got all the tact of a brick, as Mum said when she thought I wasn't listening.

"No," I say honestly, trying to flatten it.

"Bye, Mum!" says Hannah pointedly. Babs makes a "What have I done *now*?" face and goes back to the house.

It's not a competition, but I win the mums.

After a quick debate about the chances of that slug sliming to the top of the tent and falling into one of our sleeping mouths – which we have to end because Hannah's laughing and dry-retching so hard I think she might choke – we return to the all-important subject of *me*.

I tell her I'm going to stop training, and how it's actually exciting because maybe I'll find something I'm really good at – something cooler than swimming – and I immediately feel bad as she starts trying to help.

"International supermodel?"

"Yes, well, *obviously*," I say. "That's Plan B, but I'm scared of flying."

Hannah chews thoughtfully on a cube of jelly. "The thing is," she says, "you've been swimming since you were, like, eight…?"

"Seven," I correct her.

"Right. So there's so many options you haven't explored! Loads of things you could be amazing at!" She's so excited by how brilliant I'm going to be. It makes me feel tired and irritable and not very brilliant.

Suddenly a shadow looms against the side of the tent, and Hannah's dad, Damien, calls our names. He unzips the front door.

"Are you girls smoking?" He looks at us narrowly.

"No!"

"Make sure you don't, it's a filthy habit." He zips us back up and leaves Hannah and me rolling our eyes at each other. Her parents are so weird. You can't just randomly bark at your daughter, "Don't do drugs! Don't smoke! Don't get pregnant!" and call it parenting.

I laugh out loud, remembering how last month Dad thought Lavender was pregnant because she was so tearful and shifty. He very sweetly said we could cope with anything as a family.

Lav cried, hugged him and confessed she'd left her eye shadow in her jacket when she put it in the wash and now all his work shirts were glittery.

I suddenly remember I'm in the library, laughing like a loon by myself. The librarian narrows her eyes and a gang of girls stare at me as if I'm insane. I duck down behind *Swimming for Women and the Infirm* and pretend I'm engrossed. *Oh look, she's floating* and *pointing a toe. What an athlete.*

The rest of the day is OK; it doesn't get better but it doesn't get worse. I had been dreading going back to school, thinking everyone would be all, Oh my God, you came last in the time trials? But Hannah got through? That's so embarrassing for you, are you OK?

What are you going to do now? What's that coming out of your eye? *Are you crying??*

But, I hate to say it, Lav was right. No one cares. I don't think anyone even notices.

And if that makes my first day back at school sound a bit boring, then: *bingo*! That's cos it is.

I see Lavender heading towards the car park at the end of school with a gaggle of mates. I want a gaggle. I join her and give her friends a little wave as they leave, which they're too cool to return.

They're the sort of people who always make me feel sweaty and worry that I smell of food or have something between my teeth.

"How was the first day?" Lav asks.

I give a bland little *meh*.

"I was right, wasn't I?"

I have to admit it. "Yeah, no one really cares. It's not a big deal."

"*No*, about Amelia Bond's hairy face mole. She looks normal, but you know something's missing."

"Like there's a ghost on her face?"

"*Yes!*"

4

The next few days get a bit less *meh* – I make an effort to chat to people in my classes and they're not unfriendly. It's just that everyone already has friends and they're not looking for new recruits, so I spend my lunchtimes hanging out in a largely empty library. I even read the occasional book – seems rude not to – but it's not the same as having a real life friend.

By Thursday I'm thoroughly bored of eating a sandwich hidden in a book, and all morning I've been thinking about going to see Debs.

Six and a half weeks is the longest I've gone without seeing her in years, but I felt shy after the time trials. She says things like "Silver is just first place loser!" – I'm not sure how she'd treat an *actual* loser.

Plus I didn't feel I could just turn up on her doorstep

and say, "Hiya! Let's ignore the twenty-five-year age gap and hang out! You can blow your whistle at me and I'll wear a verruca sock if that makes it less weird."

There's a public pool next to my school. I've been stumping my way up this path every morning for years, with a heavy sports bag on my shoulder and sleep crust scratching at my eyes. Today I head here with my sandwich instead of the library, rubbing my eyes out of habit.

It seems empty, but I can hear some noise from the changing rooms. I wonder if it's the girls I used to train with. We weren't best friends, but after a lonely week I'd be really happy to see them now. As long as Cammie isn't there. She's rude, posh and mean. She always intimidates Hannah and me and we hate that she does.

I follow the sounds and it takes me to the girls' changing room. I push my way through the heavy door and get a big whiff of chlorine and shampoo.

The door shuts loudly behind me and fifteen half-dressed girls with wet hair go quiet and stare at me. The silence hangs, heavy and awkward and smelling of feet.

Not such an exciting smell any more. Oh, and there's Cammie. Brilliant. One foot up on the bench, moisturizing her legs, she's halfway through a story and looks up to see who's dared to interrupt her.

A couple of girls give me a small smile but they look a bit embarrassed. It's weird when semi-naked people are embarrassed for *you*.

I suddenly feel I'm not meant to be there, this isn't the welcome I'd expected. Everyone goes back to getting dressed. Cammie picks up where she left off, loudly. Following her lead, everyone ignores me.

"All right, Lou?" says a tall, muscly girl who's drying in between her toes. She says it quietly; she doesn't want everyone to hear.

One person cares! (*But I can't remember her name. Aargh!*)

"Yeah, I'm good, thanks." Mellie? Probably not, who would call a kid Mellie? It rhymes with Smelly.

"I … uh … just came to say hi. So … hi."

"Hi," says Smelly. (Mella? Maybe.)

"And also I forgot my … this. Yes, this." I'm babbling to fill the awkward silence as I open my old swimming locker and find a dusty nose clip. "Excellent," I say and pop it in my pocket.

Cammie frowns and says, "Why do *you* need *that*?"

There's a shocked silence and a couple of embarrassed giggles, swiftly muffled. (It would've been more polite to NOT LAUGH, but whatever.) My heart starts beating harder and I can feel my ears going red with anger, but I don't let it show.

"Just to block out that smell, Cammie. You reek of hair removal cream."

Zing!

Shame I only think of it before I fall asleep that night.

My actual sassy retort is to smile weakly and leave, closing the door gently behind me. Ooo, *burn*.

This place is my home, or it used to be. But clearly my pathetic performance at the time trials makes me an embarrassment to the team. Wish Lav could've seen that. Her and her "no one cares, it's not a big deal".

I seethe about how shallow they are. I'm full of rage about how the world isn't all Winners or Losers – we're all just people, guys, special snowflakes with a lot to offer the world!

To enjoy this self-righteousness I have to forget that I was *exactly* like this until a month or two ago. Lalalalalala, let's just ignore that uncomfy fact.

I head for the pool to find Debs, the closest thing I've got to a friend after Hannah. As I enter the pool area I can hear the splashing of the next swim class. These guys are younger but they're still good. I watch them dart through the pool with swift movements and slightly wonky tumble turns.

Debs is striding up and down in tiny shorts (all year round, tiny shorts – maniac) shouting at anyone who stops. You can't stop during training; your muscles cool down and you're less effective, so you've got to just power through the pain. Debs always said that was one of my great strengths.

She spots me and I wave.

She shouts something that I can't hear over the thunderous noise from the pool.

"What?" I smile and point at my ears.

"No outdoor shoes."

Um. Right.

"I'll go, then. I just came to say hi!"

She gives me a brief smile and goes back to watching the swimmers. She was never one for the soft and cuddlies, but I was expecting at least a hug, with perhaps a circling back pat at the end? (I would *like* a hug with a circling back pat at the end, dammit! I deserve one, I've had a very hard summer and she should understand that.)

She doesn't look up again, but that's cool, she's busy and I don't want to be paranoid. I sit on a bench at the back of the viewing platform and eat my sandwich. (Quickly, as the humidity makes it soggy. Bit gross.)

I try to add up how many hours I've spent at this pool: an hour a day before and after school five days a week, plus the odd lunch hour, then two hours on a Saturday morning, pretty much every week since I was seven. My mind boggles and I get out my phone to use the calculator.

I think: a) no wonder my hair is so crispy, that's a lot of chlorine, and b) I can't do maths either! What I don't know would fill a barn, as my gran would say.

I've never sat in the viewing area before. I watch the swimmers and feel drowsy at the repetitive splashing, broken up with occasional short, sharp pips from Debs' whistle. After all these years I know exactly what each sound means. "Go faster, you're slowing down, I'm watching you, keep your arms crisp, don't drag those legs! Always. Swim. Faster!"

Debs doesn't have a sound for "You're doing really well, guys, and remember it's just a sport, let's have some fun!" I snicker to myself at the thought of what that would be – a snotty squeak as she choked on her whistle.

My head droops in the warmth. It's dull watching people swim and I think about the hours my poor family spent up here on these uncomfortable benches, slapping supportive looks on their faces like they could not possibly think of anywhere else they'd rather be on a Saturday morning.

"What, the *park*? On this sunny day? You must be kidding. Let's go and sit somewhere noisy and damp. I'm happy to hug the dishwasher – or we can watch you swim *again*."

Dad and Lav can both sleep sitting up; they probably learned how to do it here.

My phone vibrates. I bet it's Hannah. I want to tell her about the girls in the changing room. Then I realize that if *she* walked in there, everyone would be excited to see her.

I stare at the water until my eyes go blurry and I force myself not to blink, when I have that unmistakable feeling that someone's looking at me. I must look demented, like I'm in a staring competition with water.

I glance over my shoulder. There's a field outside the swimming pool, and right now there's a boy in it. He's a few feet from the window but close enough for me to see that he's good-looking, small and sort of cool-without-trying. His skin is so clear he looks like a model. I finger my chapped lips.

He's kicking a ball against the wall and looking up at me while he's doing it. I'd lose a tooth to a misaimed kick if I tried that. I stare at him gormlessly.

Just then a bigger version of him walks past the door. Ah, I knew he looked familiar: he must be related to Roman Garwood. Roman is two years above me; he is basically physical perfection, and if I had more of a grasp on sex (so to speak) I'm sure I'd be feeling all sorts of rude things for him.

I don't know Roman, but I've overheard him talking to older girls and he's quite rude – blunt, and a bit prickly. (*Why* does that make him more attractive?)

Roman takes his jumper off to reveal broad shoulders and muscular arms. The shorter boy catches me staring at the aforementioned muscles and smiles. Even by this week's low standards this is embarrassing. I give him a small, no-teeth smile back.

This smile says, "Yup, I was staring at your brother like a dog at a sausage, let's never mention this again."

A third boy joins them, pulling off his jumper too, which makes his T-shirt ride up over a muscled chest. I examine my cuticles: it's hard to know where to look around here.

The *new* guy, also quite ridiculously handsome, is

fidgety; he pulls his T-shirt down, takes the ball off Small Roman and starts doing keepy-uppies. The three of them seem dejected and look like they're arguing in a half-hearted way.

Actually, I recognize that third boy! He's not at our school any more, he must be a few years older than me. But a couple of years ago, when he was still in sixth form, I had won some big county competition. I'd been messing about in the car with Mum, wearing my medal and pretending her Ford Focus was doing a victory parade for me. (You had to be there, but it was pretty LOL, guys.) I'd forgotten to take the medal off when she dropped me at school, so I sneaked in late to assembly still wearing it. This guy saw me and said something that made everyone around him stare at me and then laugh till they couldn't breathe.

I'll never know what he said – he probably wouldn't even remember – but it ruined something important to me.

Pete. That's his name.

Remembering that is the last straw for me and I shoulder my rucksack and head back to school. I doubt Debs even looks around. I keep my head down and don't talk to anyone, don't answer any teachers' questions for the rest of the day. Operation: Make Friends is on hold, possibly for ever.

I suspect this school is tragically and unluckily full of dickheads and is no place for me to find a friend. Maybe I'll just sit tight and hope Hannah flunks out of training camp.

I don't mean that.

I think I do.

She could just get a muscle injury. Not disabling, but permanent, so she'd have to give up on her dreams and I'd have someone to talk to at lunchtime. (No, *you're* selfish.)

That night Dad makes us savoury pancakes because Mum is out on another date. I lie about how well school is going (I'm sure Lav knows the truth but she says nothing) and head upstairs after watching a film with Dad.

I lie in bed listening to Lav texting and WhatsApping (so many pings!) and settle down to sleep. I can hear Mum come in. She must've had a few drinks because she's a bit loud, clattering around getting her shoes off.

I know, without even checking, that Dad was waiting up for her. She heads straight to the kitchen, immediately in full flow, ranting about her evening. Not a great date, I guess. I hear Dad laugh, the fridge clunks and there's a *tiss tiss* as two beers are opened.

I hear them chatting and laughing as I drift off. It's nice. I'm glad they're still friends. I remember when we were younger and they'd have polite conversations over our heads, Mum gripping my shoulders so tightly it hurt. I remember...

Suddenly: "Just to block out that smell, Cammie. You reek of hair removal cream" pops into my head.

And a minute later: *Melia!*

That girl's name is Melia.

Thanks, brain.

5

The next day I wake up feeling less pathetic. I'm going to have a chat with Debs. I was her favourite swimmer, I will *make* her care about me again! I'm going to catch her when she's not busy, first thing in the morning before lessons start. I head downstairs. There are four empty beer bottles in the kitchen. Mum and Dad will be grumpy this morning – glad I'm missing that.

I leave Dad a note saying I'm walking to school and head off, feeling adventurous in the chilly, damp morning.

I go straight to Debs' office, which is unlocked and has coffee cooling on her desk. Excellent: she should be back soon. I sit in a chair (although not the one behind her desk; I wouldn't dare). She takes ages. I'm stuck eyeing up her bookcase full of trophies for fifteen boring minutes. Eventually she walks in.

"There you are!" I shout.

"Aargh!" she shouts back. OK, that was a bit of an ambush.

She holds her heart and looks irritably at me as she heads to her seat and flips open her laptop.

She doesn't seem delighted to see me, which is pretty flat lemonade from a woman who threw me in the air when I won gold at the County Championships last year. No one has attempted to throw me anywhere since I was in nappies, and even then there were probably anxious people yelling, "Lift with your legs, not your back!"

"Nice summer, Lou?"

NICE SUMMER? How very dare she!

"Not great, Debs."

"Have you spoken to Hannah?"

Woohoo, someone else who wants to talk about Hannah.

"Yeah, she seems fine. Now *I*..."

"I hear she's shaved a second off her personal best in individual already. I've said if she stays focused she can almost certainly take another one off, although of course it won't be as quick as the first improvement, it never is."

She looks at me intently as she talks about Hannah.

Now I have her full attention. I feel small. I look down at my hands and pick at a cuticle.

"Aaaaanyway, Debs." (Back to me, please.) "It's weird not training every evening, I don't really know what to do with myself."

I'm hoping she'll understand and say something helpful. I look up from my hands and all I get is a view of the top of her head. She's checking her emails.

"Yeah, my last lot of burnouts said the same. I think they all got boyfriends!" She laughs as if she's said something funny. I must've missed that bit.

"I'm a burnout?" I say, noticing how wobbly my voice has gone. She finally looks up.

"Lou, are you *upset* with me?"

"No," I lie. "Are you disappointed with me?"

"No," she lies. "But your turns weren't tight enough and your backstroke was nowhere up to your usual standard – your arms just weren't strong enough on the day. So you got the result you got. You burned out. It happens."

I stare at her. "OK, Debs, only winners welcome in here, I get it." I stand up to leave, really slowly, giving her time to yell, "*LOU!* I didn't mean it to sound like that! Of course I don't care if you win or lose, we're pals. I was just being Tough Love with you because I care and I want to help you get over this."

I bend down and tie my shoelaces in silence, then retie them again, because emotional outbursts can't be rushed. Especially from a woman with the tenderness of a rock.

I finally look up and realize that she's not teetering on the edge of anything emotional, she's just checking her emails again.

Well, this first week at school has sucked, but it has taught me many things:

(1) I have no friends.
(2) This probably won't change, as no one in my class likes me (except as a tampon dartboard).
(3) I am basically uneducated.
(4) I'm *really* good at pretending I'm not about to cry.

I put number four into practice as I leave Debs' office. I don't want to enter my form room with a wobbling chin and blotchy eyes: "Damn this early autumn hay fever, right?" I don't want to go home and worry Mum and I don't want to cry in public. That just leaves the one place that still makes me feel safe.

I scoot along the corridor to the pool, head down, hoping no adult will stop me and question my loose interpretation of the school rules. I'm glad to hear nothing from the changing rooms and there's no one in the pool, so I'm left in peace to sit on one of the poolside benches and watch the steam floating over the top of the water.

I start to cry and it very quickly turns into one of those enjoyable sessions when it's a relief to let it all out and you feel so much better afterwards. I think of every sad thing that's ever happened to me and wallow in self-pity.

Once I reach our dog, Mr Hughes, who died peacefully of fat old age five years ago, it's clear I've run out of things to cry about.

After a while I subside into hiccups and dry my eyes. I root around in my bag for a tissue and find an old swimming costume, zipped up in an internal pocket and forgotten. Oh well, I think, it's not like I'll be using this again. So I blow my nose in it.

I feel much better, though I can tell that my face has already gone puffy. I'm such an ugly crier, I look like boiled ham glazed in snot.

I hear a sound across the pool and I freeze, still

holding the swimming costume/hanky to my streaming nose. Pete is lounging in the open doorway of the swimming pool; I think he's flicking away a cigarette.

I don't want him to see me covered in snot. (Admittedly, who *would* you want to parade your snotty face in front of?)

Cammie appears out of the changing rooms. She must've had extra training. She gives him an approving look.

"Waiting for me?" she asks, flirty and confident.

"Nope," he says. She smiles; he's obviously joking.

But he looks around as if the person he wants to see isn't there, then heads off down the sloping field to the car park.

Cammie looks outraged – she obviously can't believe he was so rude to her. I wonder how much angrier she'd be if she knew I'd seen that. I sit very still. *Please don't look back.*

My phone vibrates with a text, and her head whips around. She looks embarrassed but quickly recovers. If she was a cat, she'd be popping her claws out.

"Oh my god, are you *crying* over the swimming pool?" she asks with an incredulous smirk. I grab my bag and scramble for the door that Pete just left through.

It's undignified to run away from Cammie, but I can't bear being laughed at. I stumble through the door and run down the muddy slope, picking up speed as I approach the car park.

I'm running so fast now that I couldn't stop if I wanted to, which is a real shame as suddenly a Mini swings towards me as it pulls out. I try to jump out of the way but fall onto the bonnet, sliding all the way across it and landing on my feet the other side.

I'm OK! I half-laugh, half-gasp in shock, and look back at the driver.

It's Pete. His mouth is hanging open, there's a muddy smear across his bonnet thanks to Yours Truly's feet and he looks like he's going to shout at me. I do the only thing I can think of: run away again.

6

Weeeez, did you get my last email? Have you fallen
down a well or have you forgotten about me? I
miss you soooo much. I'm sorry, I don't know what
to say. I wish we'd both got in. It's cool here, but
there's no one like you. They talk about swimming
ALL THE TIME. If I'm saying that, think how bad
they must be. I'm like: Let's just look at a fox in
some wellies and chillax, guys?! Email me back!
Hxxxxx

I'm being unfair to Hannah – we usually email or text
every day. But I hate hearing about High Performance
Training Camp. I know I'm selfish, but whenever she
messages I feel a jealous sicky surge in my stomach.

I want to be a better friend than that, so on Saturday

morning I write a long email back. I don't tell her how crappy I'm feeling – I don't want her to feel guilty – so I keep it all a bit vague and bland.

The weekend passes *so* quickly. How does time move so slowly at school and then whiz past on Saturdays and Sundays? I wish I had friends to hang out with. I try not to think about what everyone else is up to or it'll make me feel too sad.

I help Dad in the garden and Mum offers to take me shopping, but I don't want to bump into girls from school – I'd feel like a social reject. Lav's stuck at home too, since she's grounded, so for most of the weekend she's reading in her room and slathering some foul-smelling muck into her hair to "bring out the shine".

Out from where?

Dad makes her sit in the back garden so she doesn't stink the house out, and she sulks on the patio for about an hour while it "sinks into her follicles". She and Dad get snappy with each other. She says if she had a *decent* allowance she could just go to the hairdresser's like her friends.

Ouch. Dad's sensitive about money. I try to give Lav a *shut uuup* look underneath her crusty hair muck but I'm too late: Dad disappears into the shed and the sounds of Radio 4 come wafting out.

All too soon I get that Sunday night feeling. Me and Lav are in the living room watching a wildlife documentary in which hundreds of little worms are darting in and out of holes on the sea bed.

"Beau Michaels," Lav says to me, unexpectedly.

I frown at her, mystified, until she pokes her tongue out in tentative, jerky little movements.

Ew! I hit her with a cushion. Lav makes kissing sound like a fight between teeth and spit where no one wins.

Mum is watching us narrowly, so we go back to watching the Beau Michaels worms, stifling our smirks. I wish I was an adult so I could just stay in the house where I feel safe, instead of having to drag myself to school five days a week.

I'm brooding on this five-out-of-seven ratio when there's a crashing noise from the kitchen. Lav and I jump. The back door has swollen in the heat so the only way to come through it is dramatically loud and fast. If we had a cat it would have a flat nose by now.

Dad marches into the living room brushing cobwebs off his shoulders. I didn't realize how long he'd been out there. He smells like Uncle Vinnie, which is a polite way of saying drunk.

It's not polite to Uncle Vinnie, obvs.

"Have you been in the shed all this time?" Lav asks.

"Yes," he says.

"Doing what?"

"Working."

She opens her mouth to say "On what?" but he leaps in before she can.

"Well, everything in the house is bloody broken, isn't it? I'm run bloody ragged trying to fix everything because you all live in squalor!" The three of us look around the spotless living room, then at each other. We have no idea what he's talking about.

"Uh, I'm sorry?" says Mum cautiously. "I just find, you know, what with breeding weapon dogs in the kitchen and all my drug dealing at the strip joint, house-work does get past me."

I try not to laugh. I know Dad's going through a tough time, but yelling at us won't help. And I *did* give him my bedroom so he could have his own space and I could live squashed between Lav's millions of bras and shoes, so – you know – a thank you might be nice.

"The lamp in the kitchen was broken!" he says accusingly. "I had to take it apart."

"Oh, is it fixed? Thanks," says Lav, to make peace.

There's a pause. "No," Dad says eventually. "It's in bits now, isn't it? Now I've got to put it together again, haven't I?"

He seems to be waiting for something.

"Thank you?" I offer.

He stomps back to the shed.

"Hide your valuables," Mum advises. "When Granny went into a home he dismantled the telly and we never got it back together. It's how he copes."

I scroll around on my phone. Nothing back from Hannah. Good – I don't want to hear any more exciting tales of training camp tonight, especially now the mood in the house has gone sour.

I feel so tired that I kiss Mum and head up to bed. Through the landing window I can see Dad's shed, a patch of light in the darkness of the garden, where now the bushes have become pitch-black, evil-looking shapes.

In the middle of the evil I can see Dad's silhouette as he sits in his shed, bent intently over whatever he's working on.

Probably taking apart a blender. It hurts my heart to watch him. He looks vulnerable, and for the first time I realize that he's getting old.

I send Han a message.

X.

She replies immediately.

X in your face.

I do have a friend who cares about me. She's just, you know, living our dreams while I rot in double chemistry.

7

The next day I wake up to the sound of Lav stretching and making agonized noises. She's so bad at mornings, I have had to put up with this drama every morning since I quit swimming. I wish Mum would just let her have espressos.

Like Lav's got anything to complain about! *I* have to have another crappy, friendless day, then another, then three more, and then it'll be the weekend and hopefully I can fake my own death or run away or suddenly become eighteen and get a job. PLAN!

Suddenly I hear a screech from downstairs. Lav and I exchange alarmed looks, then swing our legs out of bed and race out of our bedroom, pushing to get through the door first. Lav realizes her pyjamas are a bit skimpy and doubles back to make herself decent.

Mum is bent over the kitchen worktop sifting through a pile of soggy junk mail, peeling something off the back of a takeaway pizza menu. I hope *both* my parents haven't gone mad, who'll raise me? I still need so much parenting.

"Are *you* making that noise?" I ask.

"Yes!" she cries, without looking up. "Quick, get some black clothes on."

"Black clothes?" says Lav, who's inserted herself into her skinny jeans and is now behind me. "Are we doing a burglary?"

"Emergency mime?" I suggest. (Pretty pleased with that.)

"No!" Mum wails. "Your uncle …" She peers closely at the peeled-off piece of wet post.

"… Hamish, no, *Harold*, died last week. I didn't realize the funeral was today. Get dressed!"

That's *so* much information in one sentence. Lav and I are staring at each other, having a long sleepy think, when Dad enters the kitchen dressed as if he's off to work.

Mum says we have to let him if it makes him feel better.

"Who's dead?" he asks.

"Harold," says Mum. "Or Hagrid?" She squints at the blotchy ink on the funeral card. Mum has a very big family, and new uncles and cousins-twice-removed regularly crop up out of nowhere. It's impossible to keep track.

"I don't know a Hagrid," Dad muses.

"I think you've missed your chance," I point out, which makes him smile and makes me feel good.

"EXCUSE ME!" snaps Mum, looking up from her paper mush. "Is anyone listening? We have eight minutes to get out of the house and to this funeral and I'm not taking you girls in your pyjamas. Go, go, go!" She chases us upstairs.

I rush to the bathroom before Lav can get in there – she's never had a quick shower in her life. As I soap up I realize that this means a day off school! Thank you, Uncle Hester, we may never have met but you have done your loving niece a favour.

Seven minutes later we're all smartly dressed, in the car and heading for a church that Dad can't find on his phone. Lav and I are trying to dry our hair with the car heaters. It's not working out brilliantly, but Mum keeps shoving our heads down in front of the vents, insisting we need five more minutes until we're funeral-acceptable. My sore neck does not appreciate this, but any minute not spent in school is fine by me.

Dad is staring at his phone, sweeping it around in big movements. He hits me on the head but I have bigger problems, leaning between the front seats to get Lav's second-hand heater air.

The second time, however, he whacks me on my cold ear and it really hurts.

"Oi!" I protest. "Don't hit your kids."

"Sorry," he sighs, "the phone just doesn't know where we are."

"Are the gravestones not a hint?" asks Mum acidly, and we both look up to find we're driving past a cemetery towards a church. Dad looks sheepish and pockets his phone.

We have to run around the church one and a half times before we actually locate the door. We're not church people so we have no idea what we're doing. It's like when I see new swimmers come to the pool and stare at the footbath in confusion, thinking, *Is this the pool for nervous swimmers?*

We find a massive oak door that looks like our best bet. Dad pushes it and nothing moves; he just looks like he's leaning against it posing for a catalogue. After watching him lean for a while going redder and redder, we realize he needs help. The door opens slowly, and with a haunted castle-style creak we get it open about a foot. Mum and Lav slip through the gap first.

Dad pats his paunch and waves me through next. On the other side I bump into Mum and Lav, who have frozen in horror because they've emerged at the front of the church next to the vicar. They stand and smile at him like fans.

He ignores us, which is kind of weird. Does this happen to him a lot? He must be really good at vicaring.

We're looking out at a full church – there's like a hundred people here! Uncle Hebrides was *popular.* I give the room a weak smile and Dad saves the day. Taking Mum and Lav by the arm, he leads his moron family down the aisle, flashing a big, charming smile left and right at stony-faced family members while I follow trying to look like their carer.

Dad spots an empty pew near the back and pushes the three of us towards it. A woman in the row behind shakes her head at us but I can't work out if it means, *You people are terrible,* or *How sad Humphrey is dead.* We all slide along the hard, wooden bench as the vicar continues his sermon.

Then we realize what that headshake meant: *Don't*

sit there, the pew is broken! She really could've made her message clearer. But she didn't, so now the four of us are basically sitting on a seesaw. Dad shifts slightly, and Mum, at the other end of the row, wobbles as her end shoots up a couple of inches.

We all freeze and do Big Eyes at each other.

I had automatically propped my feet up on the seat in front – standard practice for a tall person facing teeny leg-room – so I take them off and try to plant them on the floor for balance. This makes the bench lurch even more dramatically and we all grab each other in panic.

Now Dad's end starts sinking; whatever the pew was resting on seems to be buckling at his end. Lav slides down towards him with a little hiss of bottom on wood. Despite my best efforts, I begin to follow her. Mum is hanging onto the other end of the pew, so she goes nowhere.

Dad is maintaining an admirably straight face as his bottom sinks lower and his knees move closer to his chin, and he manages to keep his eyes on the vicar, nodding occasionally, like: *Hmm, good point, what* is *community?*

Thankfully we're so late we've missed half the service, so we only have to sit like this for about twenty minutes. As it comes to an end the vicar tells everyone to kneel and pray, but that is not an option on the Pew of Askew so we all just duck our heads very slowly and try to look respectful.

If I shift my bum I'll flick Mum at the vicar.

People are beginning to stare. I'm staring back, I can't see anyone I recognize. Mum's family is so big. The moment the funeral is over, the mourners head for the doors. We wait for the last person to leave before we attempt to move.

"OK," says Dad. "One ... two ... three ... and up!" We all stand together. Success!

Almost.

Lav loses her footing, staggers and falls, dragging me down with her. I can't say Mum makes the tidiest dismount either. Dad helps us all up, shaking his head.

"Right," says Mum demurely, tucking her blouse in. "I think we should skip the buffet."

Dad agrees and we skulk out of a side door and into the car. I'm still shutting my door as Mum puts the car into reverse.

She's like a getaway driver.

We drive home to KISS FM; Lav called radio shotgun. I don't think that's a Thing, but Mum said not to squabble on holy ground so I let it slide.

"Who was it?" I ask Lav as she flicks through the service pamphlet she picked up on the way out.

"Hmm?"

"Who was the funeral *for*?" I ask, jiggling the pamphlet so she can't read it until she pays me some attention. "Hugo? Heathcliff? Hubert?"

She tuts and flicks to the front page.

"Violet," she snaps, and pulls it back to read. She looks up a moment later and frowns.

"*Violet?*"

Dad gives a snort of laughter. I don't understand. Lav slaps her hand over her mouth, her big brown eyes horrified. Is this a sex thing?

It's usually about sex when everyone gets it except me.

I don't see how, though. "Dad?"

Dad twists in his seat to look back at me. "Wrong church, wrong funeral."

We gatecrashed a funeral?

We sit in stunned silence.

"That's awful," I breathe.

"Don't!" cries Mum. "I feel terrible."

"So you should!" Dad says. "No one in that church was related to you and you didn't even notice!" Mum is laughing now. "I'm glad there are only four of us or you'd be getting us muddled with the pizza delivery boy!"

I realize I haven't thought about swimming in about an hour and a half, which is a new record for me. I feel quite encouraged. Maybe I am going to cheer up and get normal.

A month ago I wouldn't have believed this was possible. It's like when I had the norovirus and puked for hours until I felt like a deflated balloon. It was impossible to imagine things getting better.

However, there's still a long list of Things That Are Rubbish About Lou Brown's Life. And the latest item is: I'm not about to get a day off school cos Mum craftily stowed our school bags in the boot this morning.

She pulls up at the school gates and looks back at me.

"How is it, honestly?" she asks. Lav is fixing her make-up in the sun visor mirror.

"It's not terrible," I tell her. "It's just not what I thought I'd be doing."

Mum nods. "I understand, Lou," she says and I feel an unfair stab of temper.

"Pfft. *Do* you?" I snark.

She raises an eyebrow at me and rolls her eyes in Dad's

direction. Oh, right. I doubt anyone imagines they'll be flatmates with their ex-husband. I smile a sorry at her.

I kiss them both and slide out of the car, followed by Lav, and now we're strangers again for the rest of the day. Although, surprisingly, she walks alongside me until we're halfway across the yard before nudging me goodbye with her elbow and peeling off to sit with some friends. It's not much, but it feels sweet.

8

As I walk into school I can hear the bell ringing for the beginning of afternoon lessons. I check my timetable. Come on, PE ... please, please, PE. The only lesson I don't find completely baffling.

Unless there's a new class called Lying Down and Having a Bit of a Rest.

It's biology. Gutted.

I get there first and sit on a tall stool at the back. This is the best desk in the classroom – nearest the window, furthest from the teacher, good view of the tadpoles. Prime real estate! Someone will *have* to sit next to me.

You'd think.

Everyone enters in gaggles of twos and threes and sit somewhere they can all be together. Melia comes in and

I smile at her. But Cammie is right behind her. She spots me and mutters, "Tragic," loudly enough for me to hear. The two girls with them laugh. Melia doesn't laugh but she doesn't return my smile, either.

Biology actually passes quite quickly, as I spend the whole class thinking about my hatred of Cammie, which is strong and healthy. I get lost in daydreams of how happy I'd be if she got horrendous acne.

As we leave biology I overhear Melia and her friends talking. Apparently they've got a swimming match tonight, so the whole team is leaving straight after school in the minibus.

Interesting.

At the end of school I watch the team congregate in the car park. Debs counts them all off and they stick their sports bags and packed dinners in the boot.

It brings back memories of cheese rolls that always tasted of petrol fumes.

I grab Lav and ask her to tell Dad I'll walk home as I'll be a bit late.

"Shall I tell him you've got detention?" she asks.

"Yeah. He won't believe it, but go on."

I've never been in trouble at school. I don't think some of my teachers could pick me out of a line-up.

I put my hand in my bag and feel something silky. Excellent.

Everyone races past, keen to get out of school ASAP. If I was a teacher I'd be a bit hurt by how desperate my pupils are to leave. It's like they're fleeing a fire.

I walk against the tide, feeling a little thrill. I'm looking forward to this.

The swimming pool seems deserted, but I'm not risking it. I check all the changing rooms, even the toilets. With the exception of the occasional staff member wandering around, I have the whole place to myself.

My swimming costume is a little tighter than it used to be. I poke my stomach; I suspect that's the culprit. But as Mum always says when Lav complains about her weight: "Some people don't have arms or legs! OK?"

Can't really argue with that.

I stride towards the swimming pool and I'm about to dive in when I notice that Pete, Roman and his brother are loitering in the field *again*. They're kicking a football around and Pete is smoking.

If I had to name the person I find least relaxing to be around, I'd say Pete and Cammie are currently fighting for the top spot. But this is more my pool than theirs so

I'm determined to ignore them. They'll get bored and go away soon.

I dive in from the side and it feels amazing. I swim a length and feel the muscles in my ribs stretching. Then I lie on my back in a starfish shape and scull gently, small movements of my hands but just enough to spin me in a slow circle.

I take a deep breath and let it out bit by bit as I sink to the bottom of the pool, where I start somersaulting slowly, forwards then backwards. I can feel the air in my nose – enough pressure to stop water shooting up my nose but not enough to lose any bubbles.

I don't know what this is that I'm doing at the bottom of the pool but I've always been good at it. It's a useless trick, really, only good for making people think you've drowned. (If you need that skill regularly, then your life is more depressing than mine and I tip my hat to you.)

I start to feel an ache in my ribs and I surface slowly with my eyes closed. Mmmm. So relaxing.

I open my eyes.

Roman, Small Roman and Pete are all standing on the side of the pool looking down on me. In both ways, I sense.

The silence hangs. I say weakly, "No outdoor shoes."

"What?" says Roman.

"Nothing."

Small Roman definitely heard – he's, like, three feet closer to me than the other two.

"What were you doing down there?" asks Roman.

"Uh…"

Really, are we going to have a chat like this? I never usually feel naked in a swimming costume, but suddenly I do. I don't get out of the pool. I bob around, a little talking, floating idiot head.

I realize I need to give Roman more of an answer than "uh".

"Just floating around, really – somersaults and stuff."

"You a swimmer?" asks Pete.

I hesitate. "Used to be. Don't do it any more."

They all nod, and Small Roman smiles at me. They have no idea what a massive big deal it was for me to say that.

"Do you swim?" I ask. They don't, of course, or I'd know them. But still, Operation: Make Friends is going surprising well here, let's not derail it.

"No, we're dancers," says Small Roman. Pete rolls his eyes.

"What?" protests Small Roman good-humouredly. "We still *are*!"

"What's this?" I ask. (Lav taught me the trick of talking to boys: not too many words. It looks keen. Treat everything you say like a tweet – 140 characters or less.)

"OK, so for years we've been like this dance … uh…"

"Troupe?" I suggest.

"Collective," Pete corrects me.

Small Roman goes on. "And we just tried out for *Britain's Hidden Talent* but didn't even make it through to try-outs."

"I thought everyone tried out in front of the judges?" I ask.

"No," says Small Roman. "They're holding public auditions once a week for the next few months. We did the first one and got nowhere. You only get on TV if you're talented or mental. The people in the middle, who are just deluded and a bit pathetic, get sent home."

He looks so sad my heart breaks a bit and I scoop the water around me to fill the silence, which makes me spin in a small circle. "I'm sorry," I say sincerely, once I'm facing him again.

"Apparently people are 'over' dance collectives now there's been like a million of them on TV," explains Roman, scuffing his shoe along the floor tiles. "They said Gabe would appeal to young girls, but it didn't help."

"Uh huh," I say, sneaking a glance at Small Roman. Who I guess is called Gabe and would be appealing if I wasn't looking straight up his nose. My neck hurts.

"So we thought maybe something to do with swimming?" Gabe continues.

"Can you swim?" I ask.

It seems a reasonable question, unless they want to appear on TV wearing armbands.

"Everyone can swim," scoffs Pete.

I'm about to argue with him on that, but Gabe jumps in. "We were playing football outside and…"

"We thought you'd drowned," says Roman in a way that makes me feel a bit daft.

"But when we came in, we saw you doing that amazing underwater acrobatics," says Gabe. "It's cool."

Roman and Pete nod, and I feel a bit giddy with neckache and compliments.

"So … teach us that?" asks Roman.

"I don't want to be on TV," I lie. I do, I totally do, but

holding my gold Olympic swimming medal and smiling modestly and tearfully at the cameras, not prancing about in front of booing weirdos.

"Not *you*," says Roman bluntly. "You could train *us*."

"In … what, though? What *is* this?"

At this they all look extremely uncomfortable. They glance at each other, and I take the opportunity to stretch my neck down.

Aargh aargh aarghhh. The pain is so intense I see spots of light. By the time I look up again I think my eyes must be bulging like a squeezed hamster. (I imagine. I've never squeezed a hamster, though Hannah did once when we were eight and I didn't stop her.)

(Before you get all judgy, Mr Nibbles went on to live a full and happy life. For nine more days.)

"I guess it's kind of like … synchronized swimming," says Roman with an effort, and they all look like they're sucking a lemon. I try not to laugh. Poor boys, it must be so hard being cool all the time, eh?

"There was a synchronized swimming team from around here who got through last week's audition," says Gabe.

"But they were all girls and really hot," Pete remarks, suddenly enthusiastic.

"So hot," adds Roman, entirely unnecessarily in my opinion.

Good for them. I smooth my wet hair behind my ears before I realize how that looks. *Insecuuuure!*

"So, you want me to train you?" I ask, getting back to the point. Because although it is lovely to talk to boys about "hot" girls, *I* am getting very cold.

"Yeah. We can't pay you, though, we're broke," says Pete. From where I'm floating I'm exactly eye-level with his £150 Nike trainers and I allow myself a sceptical face.

"But we'll say hi to you at school," says Roman.

I stop treading water and sink a bit. I keep my chin underwater. My eyes feel very hot.

"*Maaate*," Gabe says to him quietly. Somehow that just makes me feel worse.

I can feel myself blushing. I swim away from them and hoist myself out of the pool on the other side. I can hear murmuring behind me. I know they're discussing if I'm upset (YES) or maybe even crying. (NO. That is water from the pool on my face. Yes, all of it.)

I *may* be a social outcast (fine, I *am*) but I don't deserve this: it's mean, and I've had a gutful of people being mean. I wanted to come and swim without

Cammie and her bitchy mates and instead I run into the male versions.

Plus, in my mind I'm already telling Hannah this story later and I want to tell her how I left in a haughty silence, so that is what I do.

9

Brilliant dramatic exit, Lou. Except ... in the changing room I realize I didn't bring a towel with me so I have to dab myself dry with toilet roll. Twenty-five minutes later, picking damp tissue clumps off my legs, I head out of the sports centre.

Why is everything so hard? I want one thing to go right. Please, just one thing. I kick the door open, and it doesn't bounce back and smash me in the face and knock all my teeth out. This is a start, though I was looking for more, tbh.

I look around. You have to be careful when you walk home alone. It's starting to get dark. I check my watch. I really didn't mean to be this late.

I've never stayed out late and lied about where I was before. I was hardly boozing at a bus stop, but still, I'm impressed by my new rebellious behaviour. For a newbie I've really committed to it; in fact I've done overtime!

Typical dweeb – Lav'll love that.

When I get in, Mum and Lav are crashed out in front of the TV. They look up at me and from their faces I guess it's obvious I had a bit of a cry as I jogged. I scoop some tears out of my ear.

"How's my goldfish?" asks Mum, patting the sofa beside her. She doesn't realize what she's just called me – my nickname from all the gold medals I used to bring home. (Not because I once pooed in the pool on a holiday to Spain when I was five, despite what Lavender may say.)

I sit beside Mum, slide down and put my head on her shoulder. When I stretch out my aching legs, they reach past Mum's feet. She nudges them with her knees. "Leggy cow," she tuts. That's nice.

We watch TV for a little while. Funnily enough it's *Britain's Hidden Talent*. I've never really paid attention to it before. The stage is huge, the contestants look tiny – I'd be terrified if that was me. There are lights zig-zagging all over it, and playing in the background is the sort of music that gets you excited in the pit of your stomach. It seems a little less bizarre now that three of the coolest boys I know would be into it.

A hefty man wearing only gold underpants prances onto the stage. Nope: *still* bizarre.

I can see it would be cool to be on that stage if you were doing something impressive, though swimming underwater wouldn't have been my first thought. How would you even get a swimming pool up there?

Boys, I think with an amused weariness. Like I've got any idea about boys.

"There's pasta in the kitchen," says Mum and I go and help myself.

"How was school?" she shouts through to me.

"Yeah. Hmm. How was your date last night?"

"Yeah. Hmm. Oh, that reminds me. Mark!"

"Yeah?" Dad shouts from upstairs. I roll my eyes. Mum never thinks that three people in three different rooms is a reason *not* to chat.

"You know Laura, who I work with?"

"No, but OK?"

"She asked me if you were single!"

Pause.

"And if I'd give her your number so she could call you."

That's so complicated. See, even old people need Facebook.

There's a silence from upstairs. Then he shouts down, "Is Laura that pretty redhead?"

Mum and Dad are a bit frosty with each other for the rest of the night. Lav and I make our excuses early and head to bed, where I tell Hannah what happened today at the pool – which is really lengthy by text. She texts back immediately.

Hey, at least you're talking to boys, right?

Always the optimist.
There are some dots on my screen; she's still typing.

Are you annoyed at them?

Yes, I reply honestly.

So ... technically, you're having BOY TROUBLE.

Ooh. That's one way of looking at it. I imagine myself at school tomorrow, looking weary, knocking back a coffee and saying to a passing sixth former, "Men! Am I right?"

Next morning, Dad drops us off early, probably

trying to get back into Mum's good books. As we're leaving, she tells him he should keep an eye out for our geography teacher, the *pretty redhead*. Zing.

"Good luck with your job interview today," I say as I get out of the car and give him a kiss. Lav gives him a fist bump.

Poor Dad, I wish I could do his interviews for him. I'd be terrible at them. He's a project manager and I can't even manage my socks into pairs, but I want to protect him from any more rejection.

I jog up the front steps of the school, past kids enjoying the sunshine before they go in. I look up and catch Gabe's eye. Of course, he's my sister's year. I don't know why I've never seen him at school before, though.

"Hi," he says.

"OK," I say.

Yes, I know. "Hi" is the word I was looking for. No one replies to "hi" with "OK".

Except this social moron.

I carry on up the steps past Gabe, pushing my Boy Trouble from my mind, and head to my form room. First lesson is English – let's see how little I know about *that* subject.

I can read and write, so it could be worse. And

actually I read quite a lot over the summer because I had nothing else to do, so this lesson isn't too bad. Which is nice, as Mr Peters is our English teacher and I'm glad that he can see there's more to me than crying on the floor covered in tampons.

At lunchtime, I attempt to chat in the canteen queue with a girl I recognize from my form. "Oh great, macaroni cheese!" I say. Come on, how could this go wrong?

She gives me a startled look. "It's basically nothing but carbs and fat, you know that, right?"

"Well," I say, feeling we've headed in a direction I hadn't expected, "you need *some* carbohydrates and fat to live."

"No, you don't," she tells me firmly. "I've got an app for that."

So she's not going to be my new friend. I think we both feel that. I find an empty table near the bins to eat alone. I act like my bread roll is fascinating: *Oh, so it's bread all the way round? I never knew.*

After a few minutes a girl in the year above approaches me and loiters by my table, looking effortlessly cool. She has a tan and is wearing loads of delicate little necklaces and bracelets that jingle when she moves.

She stands, jingling.

I sit, holding my bread roll.

"Hey," she says, like it's a bit of an effort.

I try to seem even less fussed. Well, if *that's* the game we're playing! Maybe I'll fall asleep mid-sentence.

She holds a piece of paper out towards me, subtly, between two fingers as if she's working undercover.

I stare at it. Why is she passing me a note? She raises her sculpted eyebrows at me like I'm being weird. *I'm not being weird! You're being weird!* I take the note off her and she drifts away.

I'm tempted to put the note in the bin and forget about it, but Lav says I have to be less suspicious of people at school – some of them might be nice. *I* say, pelt me with tampons once, shame on you. Pelt me twice, shame on me. (Pelt me three times, and this is why we're banned from Boots.)

Who would pass me a note, though? Unless it's Carbs Girl with a warning about this bread roll. Oh fine, I'll read it. But if it's mean, I'm *demanding* home-schooling.

Hi, this is the guy from the swimming pool yesterday. The one with the rude brother. I'm sorry Roman upset you, that was stupid – I sent a messenger in case you don't want to talk to

any of us. Can we try again? I get that it seems
weird, but this means a lot to us. We've been
dancing together since we were kids and we'd
love to be on TV together. And I think you
could be the person to help us. How about £20
a session? Know it's not much, but it's all we've
got – and a +1 to the BHT final...?
   Gabriel

Ha. Gabriel and Roman. Someone's parents knew they had a couple of winners on their hands, didn't they?

My pride is still bruised, and why does he assume I like *BHT*? What is up with that? You don't just assume everyone likes mud-wrestling, do you? Actually, I bet watching mud-wrestling is a lot less upsetting than watching an underdressed woman dance with her over-dressed dog.

But twenty quid. I do need money. I'm never going to become socially acceptable if I continue to dress like I've got the flu. Dad can't give me any while he hasn't got a job and Mum has higher bills now there's four of us (and one is busy dismantling everything we own).

Gabriel put his phone number at the bottom, so I save it to my contacts, which now has THREE boys in it (though the other two are related to me).

I text him.

OK, when do you want to meet?

It looks pretty unfriendly, but then I don't want to sound keen – I'm remembering Lav's rule. I hover my thumb over my phone, debating how to make it a bit nicer. Maybe an emoji? Probably not the poo with a smile, though it's pretty multi-purpose...

Too late, my thumb accidentally hits *send* and I watch my unfriendly message whoosh away. He replies immediately. I would've waited a while to look unfussed, but he doesn't even bother to pretend.

Brilliant! Tomorrow, 7pm at pool?

Cool. It's a date. Or, you know ... something that couldn't be less like a date if it tried.

10

Weeez! I cannot BELIEVE you're a swimming coach!
Are you the new Debs? Are you wearing teeny tiny
shorts? When the wind blows, do you feel it in your
kidneys? That's how you know they're too small.
I'm terrified about what I'm going to come home
to. New news: they get us to eat raw fish here, it's
gross!! Like eating the inside of your mouth. You
gotta try it, no calories and all protein, apparently.
Hashtag fact of the day, and you're welcome.

Han x

Aargh! It's my first underwater training thingy in half
an hour and Mum's thrown all my clothes in the wash.
Why does she do this? I run to the laundry basket in the
bathroom – nothing in there – so I hurry back to my

(*our*) bedroom, keeping a tight grip on my towel as it's currently the only outfit I've got.

Maybe with the right shoes I can style it out.

Lav is lying on her bed flicking through a magazine so shiny it's bouncing light around the room.

"Laaaaav?"

She looks up but doesn't take her headphones out.

"Please can I borrow something to wear? I've got to get to my ... job."

She languidly pulls out one earbud. "You have a job? Cool! But of course you can't borrow my clothes. Best of luck with everything."

"No, no, please!" I say before she puts her headphone back in. "Not your nice clothes, obviously, just like some sports stuff..."

"Sports stuff?" she repeats, as if she's never heard these words before but suspects they're dirty.

"Something you'd sleep in, but I'd wear out," I explain.

"Oh. Yeah, third drawer down."

She hesitates.

"Your hair?"

"Yes?"

If she says the word "pubic" I. Will. Cry.

"Come here," she says, reaching on to her shelf for a

pot of oil. She pours a little drop into her hands, stands in front of me and starts smoothing it gently through my hair. This is all very surprising.

"Thanks, Lav, this is … nice of you."

"It's good to see you cheer up, instead of lying on your bed pretending you're not crying."

"Sorry about that."

"I was going to start hanging fairy lights off you to lighten the mood, but I thought you'd electrocute yourself with tears."

I stand silently while she massages oil into my hair. Me and Hannah used to make fun of Lav behind her back for being ditzy and "boy-centric", as a teacher once said. But if these last few weeks have taught me anything, it's that I am *not* the brains of the family.

My head and face burn hot and the rubbing isn't really helping. It's like Lav is determined to bring all my shame out in one massive blush.

"Thank you!" I say, pulling away from her before my head explodes.

"That's OK," she says. "We'll sort out your hair this week, then work on your skin."

She has a way of making me feel like an old car she's going to fix up.

I run downstairs and out the front door. Mum calls something as I slam it behind me. It didn't sound like "good luck" – oh no, wait, it was "don't slam the door".

Whoopsy.

I run down the road and up the embankment towards the swimming pool. I've run this route so many times I could get there with my eyes closed, though I don't try it. I don't want to get hit by a car before Lav's "worked on" my skin.

Life is full of surprises, I muse, and a sudden draft around my midriff proves me right. My top doesn't reach my trousers. This is the last time I borrow Lav's clothes.

As I run I feel an unfamiliar sensation … it's my hair bouncing! It's never bounced. *Crunched*, maybe.

I round the corner, hurdle over a few flowerbeds and burst into the swimming pool to the sound of cheering. I wheel around to see what I've interrupted. Is there a race on? But no, it's the three boys, cheering *me*!

"Here she is!" announces Gabriel.

That is such a great way to enter a room. I beam. Then I dial the beam down a little. *Don't be too keen, Louise. Be cool.*

I cough. I am cool.

"See you at the bottom," says Roman, pulling his

tracksuit off. I blush. I am so pathetic. (Roman said "bottom" at me! Ha ha. I'll tell Han.)

"Not yet!" I assert, fiddling with my rucksack to hide my blush. "I need to see how strong you are as swimmers before we start doing anything underwater."

"Why?" asks Pete brusquely.

I look at him hard. Maybe it's the run, maybe it's the fact that my hair bounced, or maybe it's the cheering, but I feel some of my old confidence return.

"Because while some people like to believe that 'anyone' can swim, they can, in fact, be wrong."

Pete doesn't say anything but looks like he's biting back a nasty remark.

"And sorry, I don't know your name...?" (I do know his name. I am being extremely petty. But it's *fun*. And I haven't been splashing around in much fun lately, so I deserve it.)

"Pete."

"OK, *Pete*," I say, bouncing a little on the balls of my feet and feeling like a mini-Debs. I can see Gabriel stifling a smirk behind him. "I'm Lou and I'm in charge of you while we're in this pool. And I don't want you to drown. So I need you to show me that you can swim. Please."

Pete sighs and slides into the water.

"I've been swimming for years," he scoffs. "I'm probably faster than you. Don't get weird about it, but men are stronger than women, you have to admit."

"Excuse me," I tell him, and grab my rucksack and head for the changing room.

As I push through the door I can hear Gabriel say, "Stop being rude to her. If she goes we've got no one else."

I march back out of the changing room a few minutes later wearing my swimming costume. I step up on the diving block and look down at them. "Four lengths, front crawl?" I snap on my swimming cap.

"Uh…" Gabe begins.

"Nope!" I beam at him. "Time to race."

They all step up on diving blocks beside me and I nod at the minute clock.

"Let's go at twelve." I watch the second hand slide towards the top and then dive, hard. It feels a little unfamiliar, sensations you forget about like the feel of water slapping against your armpit. I'm slower these days but still faster than three cocky civilians. Probably. *Hopefully.*

I start to feel winded on the third length but I think

of Pete scoffing at me and push onwards. Finally I slap my hands against the side of the pool and lift my head. I'm aware that no one is next to me and I get a stomach-lurching fear that they finished ages ago and are already out of the pool, playing keepy-uppy with a float or texting their girlfriends. Unsportspersonlike!

But I hear splashing behind me and my stomach unknots. After a few long seconds, Pete slaps his hands down beside me, Roman a moment later on the other side. Roman, panting hard, looks genuinely impressed. Pete even manages a rueful *whatever* shrug. I smile. Normal service has resumed.

We turn around, wiping water out of our eyes and ears, and watch Gabriel swimming towards us. He's just started the final length – he's not a bad swimmer but he's slow and clearly exhausted. I don't feel like being cocky any more.

"He's been ill," says Roman suddenly.

"What?"

"Gabriel. He had ME for years, you know ME?"

"Is that when you're tired all the time?"

"Yeah. Sometimes he didn't leave the house for months."

So that's why I hadn't seen him before.

"It's amazing he's back in school, but he's not very fit," Roman goes on.

This is an understatement. We have time for quite a lengthy medical conversation while Gabriel finishes the race.

"Is this going to be OK?" Roman says, looking from Gabriel to me as if I have all the answers.

"Yes," I lie.

I don't know what they're trying to do, I don't know if it's even got a name or if it's just Drowning to Music. But I'm involved now, and as I watch Gabriel swim on his final lap I know I'll do whatever I can to make this work for him. Them, I mean.

Gabriel reaches the edge and staggers to his feet. He can barely breathe and he's red in the face but he's smiling. "You've no idea, but that's good for me," he pants.

"That's good for me, too," I lie. I'm getting better with practice. "Easily good enough! Yep!"

11

We all dry off, put sweatshirts on and have a talk about what they want to do. They show me some of their dance moves. If anyone walked in right now, it would look like they were showing off to try and impress me. Tragically, no one does.

People only walk in on me when I'm crying or tidying up tampons, apparently.

The boys are really good: Pete and Roman can do a load of strength holds and flips, and Gabriel is less strong but he's bendy and wiry. I can see them doing this as kids, Pete and Roman as best friends for years, letting Roman's little brother join in. Even Pete seems less intimidating when I imagine him as an eight-year-old landing on his head after another backflip turns into a backflop.

As they bounce around on their hands, it turns into a competition between Pete and Roman. I get the feeling most things do. I watch while their faces go redder, but they both refuse to give up first. Gabe stretches out a cramp.

"Did they say anything else ... the try-out guys?" I ask, mainly to distract them so one of them will fall over and we can get back to training.

"Just that they had enough dancers," Pete says in an upside-down gasp.

Gabe and I look at each other. OK, it's not the most helpful advice.

"And," comes a voice from under Roman's sweatshirt, which is currently sliding down his torso and revealing... Ahem, never mind. "They said that we had a strong look."

Pete slowly topples over into the armband box.

"Careful!" I call over. "They're covered in verruca plasters."

Pete scrabbles out of the squeaking pile making retching noises, while Gabe and Roman laugh. I don't think I've ever been funny in front of someone who wasn't family or Hannah. I always feel hilarious *inside*, the message just never seems to get out.

"So." Pete turns to me, rubbing his neck. "You don't know what you're doing, then?"

I stand up for myself. "Pete, dancing underwater isn't a Thing. I'm happy to help, but it's synchronized swimming without all that pesky breathing. Have you any idea what you'll perform in?"

"Swimming trunks," says Gabe promptly. "Ideally?"

Pete ignores this, though it makes Roman laugh.

"My dad works at the aquarium," he says, like it's obvious. "They have these spare tanks and we're going to borrow one."

"OK," I say slowly. "By 'spare' you mean..."

"In an unlocked warehouse."

"And by 'borrow' you mean..."

"Well..."

"*Steal?*"

"Don't be dramatic."

"Well, I can't see any problem with that plan at all. Great stuff."

I rub my stomach, which has clenched hard at that news. Like I don't have enough to worry about. An ill swimmer, a grumpy one and one I'm too shy to look at; a sport I think we're inventing on the spot; a local team already through to the final (and they're "really hot", so woohoo for them) ... and now we'll be performing in a nicked tank that's probably full of old fish poo.

I reach for my phone to google "illnesses from fish poo".

"Sorry?" Pete is looking pointedly at my phone. "Have you got time for that?"

He's right. Rude, but right. I need to concentrate, we have *a lot* to do.

The boys slide back into the water and I put thoughts of fish poo to one side. I've made a playlist for their training sessions. I was up all night choosing songs that were cool, but – you know, not *too* cool; not self-consciously cool. But still cool. (It was as exhausting as it sounds.)

I rub my tired eyes – they feel like boiled eggs – and pop my iPhone into Lav's portable speakers. (I did ask her permission. Very quietly ... when she was in another room.)

"I've made a playlist, guys!" I announce to the group. It's hard teaching people who intimidate you; you find yourself calling them "guys!" quite a lot. I press *play* and get them to do some leg stretches while they tread water. I watch their faces for any early signs of sneering, but no one even mentions the music. It must be OK.

School has taught me that people make fun of you when something is lame and stay silent if it's acceptable.

"Hey," says Gabe, "you've got great taste in music."

"Thank you!" I casually push back my fringe in a gesture far more suited to Lav, but hey ho.

I ask them to sink underwater a little to see if they can lie a foot beneath the surface without panicking. Most people struggle with that. Roman and Gabriel get it quickly, but Pete is a massive control freak and keeps thrashing about. I tell him it's really hard to master, which seems to wave a flag on a temporary truce between us.

While they're practising sinking, I get dressed and then come back to stand at the side of the pool. I have the guys treading water and lifting their arms up to test their strength – and, yes, *maybe* I have found a whistle and *perhaps* it does give me a mild feeling of power. But it's the only way to get their attention when they're underwater. Honest!

Suddenly the doors bang open and Debs strides into the pool area. (Can't she ever just *walk* anywhere? And put some trousers on.)

I look down at the outfit I borrowed off Lav. It's about as small as what Debs is wearing. This is my new look:

half-naked stalker. I quickly hide my whistle under my T-shirt, not that it offers much coverage.

Debs is followed by Cammie, Melia and two other girls I know from swimming, Nicole and Amanda. If I was that pretty (and I can't lie, they all look like a bloody shampoo advert) I would think I could find it in my heart to be a nice person. But Cammie, Nicole and Amanda are all actively mean – not just to me, to everyone. Melia is neutral; she doesn't stop them, but she isn't horrible herself. I'm not sure if that makes her a good person.

The boys immediately drop their arms and start swimming about as if they're just having a casual swim: nothing to see here, no biggy, guys. Which is great, except now I'm standing on the edge of the pool *watching them* like a total weirdo.

"Hey, Pete," says Cammie archly.

"All right," he replies.

"Not bad, yeah," she says, totes unfussed.

The three girls watch this incredibly boring back-and-forth with looks on their faces, like: *What's going on here? Cammie and her exciting love life, eh?*

Debs takes in the scene, a wry smile on her face. "OK, Louise?"

"Yes, thank you, Deb-or-ah," I say tightly.

"Just watching boys, are you?"

Debs looks down at my outfit and her lips move as if she's about to say something else, but she refrains. She's got that Pete thing where you always think a withering put-down is just around the corner.

It's so unnerving, like being trapped in a car with a wasp.

Would I have ended up like that if I'd got through to the Olympic training camp? Is Hannah going to? It makes me glad I didn't get... Hmm.

No, if I'm honest with myself I'd still rather be a horrible cow with a gold medal. I could always go into therapy later and sort myself out.

"Are you coaching them for something, Lou? Good, good, fill the days."

"*Coaching* them?" I ask, stuffing down my rage and faking complete confusion. "For what?"

Deb's eyes narrow. "So what *are* you doing?" she asks carefully.

"Just swimming," says Gabe and swims a little circle to demonstrate. He is a terrible liar. We'll leave him at home the night we nick a fish tank.

Debs still looks suspicious.

I panic and say, "I'm just hanging out here out of habit, really. I miss swimming." Apparently the best lies have a grain of truth in them.

There's a silence, then Debs carries on walking towards her office, followed by the four girls. I feel a temporary sense of victory – she's backing down, she's leaving us alone! This is amazing! Take that, Debs, you and your stupid girl gang. She shuts the door like a full stop.

I turn back to the boys with my most Unbothered Face.

"*Pfft*. Don't even know why they're here, there's no swimming training tonight."

"No," says Pete, hanging off the side of the pool and re-adjusting his goggles, "that's the swimming team that's already through."

Hot sick jumps at my ribs.

"What, the *BHT* team?" I croak, feeling my Unbothered Face fall off. Now where's my Extremely Bothered Face...?

"Yeah."

"*Argyhjfffgggh!*"

"You OK, Lou?"

"I am *fine*. Everything is *fine*. When's the next public try-out?"

"This weekend."

"*This weekend?*" Here's my Extremely Bothered Face: I'm wearing it.

"Yeah," says Gabriel calmly. "It's up north. There's weeks more of try-outs, and it's another five weeks before they come back to this part of the country, so it's cool."

Depends on your definition of "cool".

"Five weeks isn't very long," I grumble.

"Well. It's a hundred quid to you," says Roman reasonably.

"Are you paying me per session or per week?" I ask cheekily. Pete and Roman look at me stony-faced. Gabe watches with mild curiosity.

"Because the note said per session..."

They say nothing.

"Per week it is, then," I agree. (Wooohoo! A hundred quid!)

"Seems reasonable," I chat to myself as I pack up my sports bag. (Wheeeeeeee!! That's SO MUCH MONEY!!!)

"Are you off, then, now you've earned your money for today?" asks Roman. I can't tell if he's teasing.

"I'm not allowed out past nine on a weeknight. My dad's coming to get me," I say, truthfully.

Pete and Roman seem to find that funny, I don't know why.

"So between now and the next session you'll come up with a routine?" says Roman. Somehow he manages to make it sound more like an order than a question.

"Ab-so-*lute*-ly." I give him a big fake-calm smile.

An … underwater synchronized swimming routine. Yes. I'll just come up with one of them, then. *Easy*.

"I'll work out a routine and then we'll try it next time we meet and hopefully you won't drown."

Gabriel laughs, Roman smiles. Pete ignores me.

12

The boys stop to get something from the vending machine and I don't want to look socially clingy so I go and wait outside. My phone dings: a message from Hannah.

> Did YOU know bananas were fattening?! Get outta town! I LIVE OFF BANANAS! :-(

Dad pulls up in Mum's car.

"*DAD!*"

"What?"

"You know *full well* what."

He's just wearing pyjama shorts with a coat thrown over the top. He's even still got his slippers on.

"I look normal from the outside," he says. "You can

only tell if you're right next to the car and look in and down."

"Bye, Lou," say Roman, Pete and Gabriel as they walk right past the car, looking in and down.

"Oh dear," grins Dad, "have I made you look uncool?"

"*Yes*, actually," I tell him, "so don't smirk at me like it's no big deal because that's exactly what you've done. I've got zero friends at school, just two and a half acquaintances" (given the mild bubbling hostility off Pete I won't consider him a whole acquaintance) "and you've just embarrassed me in front of them. So you can stop smiling about it."

"Louise, being popular isn't about trying to be cool," says Dad.

He has *no* idea how wrong he is. This is exactly the sort of terrible, awful, useless advice you get off people over twenty-five. I've heard it a million times, along with how I'll be pretty when I'm older and one day I'll regret shaving my legs. (When? When I want to stuff a duvet cheaply and need all that thick leg fur? I *don't* think so.)

"You know, being popular," says The Man Who Doesn't Get It, warming to his theme, "is about doing what *you* like."

Why doesn't he just tell me to be myself?

"Just be yourself. Do what makes you happy, and then everyone will see how cool you are and want to be friends with *you*!"

"OK! Thank you so much, Dad, I really appreciate that you care, especially as you've got so much on your plate at the moment, but this is terrible advice. Being cool is *not* about being yourself, it's *not*, and you need to stop handing out that advice in case one day someone actually listens to you and you ruin their life. I *am* myself and I have *one* friend, who emails me details of meals! And my school days are *so* lonely and it's not fun. You have no idea what it's like to be lonely. I'm sorry, but no."

There's a silence.

"It's lonely being unemployed," says Dad.

I rub my finger along the door handle and stare at the chocolate wrappers on the floor.

He takes a deep breath. "You wake up and you have nowhere to go and everyone rushes off to school and work, where people notice if they're not there and where people need them, while I sit at home and email people asking them to notice me or need me, and no one does. That's unemployment. If you don't like school, Louise, at least it will end soon and you'll make new friends somewhere else. But *I* don't know when this will end."

We stop at some traffic lights. On impulse I grab Dad's hand.

"*We* need you!" I tell him. "Me and Lav and Mum, we all need you, and we like having you around. Look, you and Mum are divorced and she's still happy to live with you, think how amazing that makes you! And I'm having to share a room with Lav and all her girl … smells … and glitter that gets *everywhere* and spiky boot things, and I'm still happier that you're here."

"Thanks, Lou," he says.

My palm sweats gently.

"Shall we stop holding hands now, Dad?"

"Yeah, I need to change gear."

Someone behind us beeps loudly: the lights have gone green.

"Do you mind?" Dad yells. "We're bonding and we're new to it!"

We drive home in silence. But a nice silence.

I text Hannah.

Then why aren't monkeys fat?

13

08:48

Hey guys, we're going to hang out before the tournament next weekend. If the weather's nice we'll go to that park near the leisure centre – let's meet at the fountain at 1?

Cammie xx

08:51

Sorry, Lou! I forgot to take you off the group email for the swim team! Ignore this, see ya around.

Cx

The next morning is Saturday and Mum is making eggy bread. She calls it French toast, but I can't see why dipping something in egg makes it French. It puts me off the idea of French fries. I share this thought with the kitchen.

"Yes, and French letters," agrees Mum. Dad laughs explosively. Lav and I frown and google that on our phones.

"Ew, Muu-um…" says Lav, who has a better phone and gets the answer first.

"Dad was saying you've made some new friends," Mum says to me brightly. *Thanks, Dad.*

"Well." I'll summarize it for her. "I am employed by three people too cool to be my actual friends."

"Oh, come on!" she scoffs. "My Lou doesn't care what people think of her." So very incorrect.

"No, I just dress badly. Which makes it look like I don't care, but I do. If I had some cash I'd buy some new clothes and then you could see how badly I care about what people think of me."

Lav nods, backing me up, then goes back to her phone.

"Not that I need cash," I say hastily for Dad's sake. "Because material things like money aren't as important as, like, family, and love and that. Plus I'm earning twenty quid a week coaching these three."

"I can't believe you've got a job before me!" says Dad,

120

poking me in the shoulder. "What are you coaching them in?"

"Burlesque," I tell him. He blinks at me.

"*Swimming*, obviously!"

"That's nice. I bet you're good at that. So, your new friends. What are their names?" Mum persists.

I give in and tell them. "My *employers* are called Roman, Gabriel and Pete."

"What?" says Lav, putting down her phone. "How are you friends with *them*?"

She suddenly realizes how rude that sounds.

"No, I mean … the thing is. OK, ha, what that *sounded* like…"

"I know, Lav, I'm just helping them out with something."

"You should get them to say hi to you at school, though," she suggests. "If people think you know them you'll have a better chance of making some friends. That's why Becky used to play cards with Pete's gran when she did work placement at the residential care home."

"Lavender! That's a terrible thing to say!" exclaims Mum.

We both look at her and try to work out which bit she means.

"No, Mum, it's true," I say. "Now Hannah's gone I haven't got anyone to hang out with."

"Which is not her fault," Lav informs Mum.

"It is a *bit*," I say gloomily.

"Why don't you 'hang out' with each other?" Mum asks.

We look at her as if she's suggested we grow tails.

"Anyway. It's because you always had Hannah," Lav continues. "You didn't know she'd just disappear one day to Swim Team School."

"High Performance Training Camp," I correct her, but quietly.

"And school is stupid." She looks very adult all of a sudden. "You know who your school friends are?"

"Invisible Girl and Non-Existent Boy?"

She ignores this. "They're people who *happen* to be your age who *happen* to live near you. So you end up in the same class and that's who you've got to choose from. Just sit tight a few more years and then there's a whole world out there of people you'll like more."

We all sit and digest that.

"Well," says Mum. "Lou has a job and Lavender's become a philosopher." She looks at Dad and shrugs. "I guess our work is done. I don't know about you, but

I'm going to hang around outside Maccy D's and take selfies."

"Nice for some," says Dad, getting up from the table. "I've got to get my nails done for Prom and I have literally *nothing* to wear!"

Lav and I roll our eyes. They think they're so funny.

"I don't take selfies," I inform them sniffily.

"Yes," says Lav, not really helping. "And I don't wear acrylics – they're so bad for your natural nail."

14

Lou

Guys, click on the link, could we do this move?

Pete

I could.

Roman

We could if we had gills. Seriously, Lou?

Lou

Sorry, sorry, just a thought.

Pete

Are you having trouble with the routine?

Lou

No!! Course not, no. LOL.

Gabe

Hey guys, what did I miss? I was washing my gills.

Lou

Ha ha.

Gabe

Don't make fun of my gills.

Roman has created a WhatsApp group for me, him, Pete and Gabe. When it first popped up on my phone I was sitting in the canteen by myself and I went bright red. Cammie would kill to be WhatsApping Pete and Roman every day. If only she *knew*. Ha!

I hug my smugness to myself. I wish everyone knew.

I watch her holding court on her table of girls, her shiny ponytail swooshing with every overdramatic gesture. She feels me looking at her and turns her head to fix me with a challenging stare.

Stop staring at me, you lesbian, she mouths.

I go red again and return to being very interested in

my lunch. *Aha, Ms Bread Roll, we meet again.*

Sod Cammie, I still feel smug. Though less smug when Roman and Gabe walk past and completely and utterly blank me. I look up at them with a friendly smile that I turn into a cough, then a grimace and finally some choking on bread.

So I sort of have friends, but they're secret friends, too ashamed to acknowledge me in public. Cool, that's cool.

It's a tricky week. I spend every lunchtime and evening googling synchronized swimming, but it all looks so boring. I wonder what Debs' team are doing, but I know there's no way I could spy on them. Cammie seems to have Lou-radar: I spend most of my time trying, and failing, to be ignored by her.

Every time I finish on the school computer I dump my cache. The last thing I need is to be outed as some sort of synchronized swimming obsessive. During lessons I doodle ideas in my notebook and try to think like Hannah. Constant optimism! Maybe underwater synchronized swimming *is* a Thing. It's just a new Thing.

New things always look weird to begin with. Imagine being the first monkey who grew a thumb. No one realized how useful that was going to be – they probably all ran around yelling, "Look at Clive's hand! It's icky, hit it with a rock!" Thousands of years later, we're texting with it and Clive has the last laugh.

By the end of the week I'm so obsessed with synchronized swimming routines that at dinner I stick six runner beans in a pile of mash and imagine they're legs. I'm up all night with my phone in my mouth, using it as a torch to light up my notebook as I scribble in it. Lav has made several 2 a.m. death threats but I argue, quite reasonably, that now I'm frightened to turn the light off in case she sneaks up on me.

I don't have time to juggle everything, and find I'm having this conversation a lot:

"Louise, where is your homework?"

"Ah … is it not in the pile on your desk?"

"No, because you didn't put it on my desk, so if it was on my desk that would be spooky, wouldn't it?"

"Hahahahaha, that's funny, Mr P. Great stuff."

"Louise?"

"Hello, yes?"

"Give. Me. Your. Homework."

Teachers always used to give me extra time to do my homework, because between training and travelling to competitions I only had my morning breaks to scribble out something. Now I'm working even harder, but because it's secret I have to do my homework too.

Not to sound like a Classic Teenager here, but seriously, *so* unfair. Fascists.

And I *am* trying – I hate being the densest person in my class. I stick my hand up for every question (I mainly get them wrong, but hey, good arm exercise, right?) and take loads of notes in class, even if my books are covered in long, jagged scrawls where I fall asleep mid-word.

A week after our first training session I meet the boys for another one after school. They all seem pretty excited. Even Pete's eyes light up as I pull my A3 notebook out of my rucksack, open it carefully and hold it up for them to admire.

In places I've had to sellotape extra pages into it to make a bigger canvas for my designs. I feel like a mad scientist unveiling some freakish experiment – "Behold! I have bent the laws of nature to my own demonic will!!" (*Maniacal cackling.*)

The boys stare at it in silence. I feel my smile falter. Do they not like it? Maybe it's not ambitious enough. Did I draw Gabriel too small? I should've just put *G*, *R* and *P* on their heads.

Roman looks at me, opens his mouth, frowns and closes it again. He goes back to scrutinizing the notepad.

"Lou," Pete says with typical grace and politeness, "what the f—"

"It's amazing!" Gabriel jumps in, loudly.

"Thanks." I beam at him.

"It's just … what is it?"

Really? I thought it was perfectly obvious. I take them through it, patiently.

"Here's the three of you…"

"Am I the one with the big ears?" Pete interrupts.

"Yes."

"And I'm the little one?" Gabe says.

Definitely should've just put *G*, *R* and *P* over my stick men.

"Um, yes. Now this is the three of you doing a twist dive in from the side, then barrelling down to the bottom, where you form a circle."

"Form a circle how?" asks Roman.

"Hold your ankles! Now, *here's* where it gets a tad tricky…" I'm engrossed in my diagrams and only look up when I realize they're not crowding around my notebook any more. They're all bent double.

"Are you … being sick?" I ask.

"I can't touch my toes!" gasps Gabe.

"Yours are a lot nearer than mine, mate," pants Pete.

Roman straightens up. "We can't touch our toes," he asserts, as if it's *my* fault.

"Really?"

"Well, touch yours, then," Pete challenges me.

I bend, wrap my fingers around my toes and stand up. Honestly, call themselves dancers?

"Don't worry," I say. "Bodies are bendier in water."

"Are they?" Of course it's Pete who challenges me. I blow my whistle at him.

"Yes." (I have no idea.) "Everyone in the water and let's try it out!"

They line up along the edge of the pool, looking dubious. I stand on a bench and demonstrate a twist dive as best I can. They all nod.

"Three... Two... One... *Dive!*"

Let me say right here and now: I thought they could do this routine.

I swear I wasn't trying to make them look stupid, as Pete suggests afterwards through a bloody tissue (Roman kicked him in the face). I wasn't trying to kill anyone either, though I accept, if that had been my aim, I'd have been pretty happy with how the evening went.

But I'm not happy with it, I'm quietly devastated. I sit on a bench at the side of the pool as Pete lists off the many reasons why he wants this week's twenty quid back. He twists a tissue up his nose to leave both hands free for gesticulating. My stupidity demands a lot of hand gestures, apparently.

I bow my head and mutter "sorry" every time he pauses for breath.

"All right, that's enough." I didn't notice Roman come back from the toilet. He's finished being sick now. (Gabe accidentally headbutted him in the stomach.)

Gabe isn't unharmed either. I hadn't really factored in enough places to breathe, so he got dizzy and had to be fished out of the pool.

There's a silence. I seize the opportunity. "I thought you were better swimmers!"

Three pairs of eyes swivel towards me. The mood isn't friendly.

"OK. I didn't mean it like I'm blaming you. I honestly thought it would be good. I'm really sorry."

My voice cracks and trails off. I feel a tear slip down my cheek.

"I can come up with an easier routine! I mean a better one. A *better* one." I'm begging them now. No one is looking at me, not even Gabe. I pick up my rucksack and head for the door.

I walk slowly, giving them time to calm down and stop bleeding and retching long enough to say it's OK, let's try again.

When I finally reach the door, *still* no one has said, "Come back, Lou! Sorry we're lame swimmers! This is all our fault, now we think about it, but please could you give us an easier routine for our feeble abilities?"

First Debs, now them. People are hard-hearted round here.

I sit on the grass verge for twenty minutes waiting for Dad. The boys don't come out in that time, which is a shame cos I'd sat on the ground so I'd look pathetic and sad.

Dad's car pulls into the car park and I stagger stiffly to my feet, brushing wet grass off my bum. I get in the passenger seat.

"Daa-aad..."

"He turns a worried face to me. "What?"

"I think I got *sacked*."

He lights up with sympathy. "It sucks, doesn't it?"

"It sucks so much!"

"You feel really embarrassed, but angry, too."

"Right! I *know*..."

"And the surprise, that makes it worse."

132

"Totally does."

We bond all the way home about being treated badly. We agree that we are the most unappreciated, brave people we know. We pull into the driveway. Dad turns off the engine and sits, looking like he's thinking carefully about his next words.

"When you get *dumped* dumped," he says slowly, "it's even worse because they may well have seen you naked."

"That would be so much worse!"

"Yes, it is. If someone who has seen your bum rejects you, it's extra hurtful."

"I'm never going to take my clothes off in front of *anyone*," I say emphatically.

We get out of the car.

"Wait, Dad, was *that* the sex talk? It was a bit brief."

"It was efficient! In ten seconds I turned one of my girls into a nun."

"Ha. Good luck with the other one."

15

You got dumped?! Weez, you're having proper Boy Trouble now. Are you honestly never going to take your clothes off in front of anyone? I guess you won't have to buy matching underwear, so there's a saving! Your mum said when she joined match.com she bought so much lingerie they knew her by name in Bravissimo!

HANNAH! I have to wash my brain now!

Sozzlecopters. Forget I ever said that. How are your folks?

Good. Think I'll keep them. How are yours?

Ugh. If I find a receipt, I'm getting a refund. SO
MUCH PRESSURE! If it wasn't for you and Candy
Crush I'd chuck my phone and get some peace.

I trudge into school the next day feeling like I've got
DUMPED written on my forehead. Typical, Dad drops
me off just as Roman and Gabe's mum does the same.
Displaying the sort of perfect timing they can't achieve
in a swimming pool, I think, and smirk meanly.

They don't say hi. No matter, they never did anyway.
Gabe and I make eye contact and he gives me a fleeting
smile. Between him and Melia, I've got two secret, silent
"friends". My birthday party will be quite the riot.

I take my phone out – nothing. Hannah and I are
chatting a bit more, but there's nothing on WhatsApp.
Dad's sent me a photo of his most recent job rejection.
"Dear Murk," it begins.

Only the coolest people get dumped, Dad writes
underneath. Lots of love and best wishes, Murk Brown.
(Do I sound like a paint colour?)

As in, "We're going to paint the toilet Murk Brown"? I
reply.

I sit by myself in physics. Operation: Make Friends is
on hold for now. For once I don't mind having no one to

talk to, I'm not in the mood to chat. I get out my physics book and doodle on it a list of reasons why it's for the best that I'm not working with the boys any more:

(1) I don't have to worry about being cool in front of them. (Hanging out with these boys is stressful – I always worry I'll reveal how lame my life is when they talk about parties and I have nothing to contribute except the funny thing that happened when me and Mum went to the car wash. A dog walked through it and came out soapy, it was hilarious and I tell it well, but it's a tragic insight into what I do on a Friday night.)

(2) More free time? (Oh, whoopee.)

(3) No more money. (Hmm. More space in my wallet??)

Once morning lessons are done, I head off to the canteen. Standing in the queue I notice that Melia is behind me, and without Cammie for once.

I decide to turn around and smile at her, and if she smiles back I will upgrade this smile to a chat. Then from a chat we'll move towards eating lunch together. Then we'll just be a hop, skip and a jump from a sleepover!

Then we'll kick Cammie out of school and everyone will be happier without her. (Cue music and balloons.)

OK, better not get ahead of myself. First I have to trick Melia into chatting to me and enjoying my company. I swivel round and realize I'm too close, like I'm swooping in for a kiss.

I step back and open my mouth to say "Hey!" or "How's it going?" or "What's up, dawg?" (Probably not the last one).

But she's looking down at her phone. I know she's seen me turn around for this brilliant chat we were about to mutually enjoy, but she's blanking me.

I bet she's scared Cammie or Nicole or Amanda will see us talking and make fun of her. I *bet* that's it. I can even see her glance around the canteen for them. I bet they had a go at her for saying hi to me in the changing room the other week. Argh! Where do people get off being such mad control freaks?

Whatever. I'm going to have this chat whether she likes it or not, she can't ignore me. (She can ignore me. This could get extremely awkward.)

"How's it going?" I say.

"Cool."

"Great stuff. Bit of a queue *again*."

"Yeah."

This is like milking a tortoise. No, blood from a stone; that's the saying.

"Any plans this weekend?"

"Not really."

I persevere, but it's like she's holding up a big Banter shield. She deflects my chat with things like "nightmare" and "classic" while I babble on, and everything she's saying means *nothing*. I get the distinct feeling she'd walk off if she wasn't waiting for food.

"What you going to do, eh?" is the most I manage to get out of her before she goes back to looking at her phone. I stare at the top of her head for a few minutes, then get distracted by something awful happening on the other side of the cafeteria.

Roman is talking to Cammie.

Not flirting: actually talking. She's nodding and he's gesturing at Gabriel, who's standing back like he doesn't want to get involved, and I have a sudden – possibly mad – fear that he's replacing me.

I feel so angry and jealous. Before I know what I'm doing, I leave the queue and I'm striding towards them. Gabe looks up as I approach and the surprise on his face brings me back to my senses before I march over there and bounce Roman and Cammie's stupid pretty heads together.

So, what I actually do is blush bright red, march towards the most popular people in my school looking like a beetroot-faced killer, then at the last minute skip round them and run out of the cafeteria.

Even before the doors swing closed I can hear a sudden gale of surprised laughter.

"What was *that*?" a boy hoots, and I march down the corridor with no idea where I'm going. I'm just embarrassed and I want to be by myself.

Back in the library. My old Plan B. Except this time I don't even have a sandwich to hide in my book.

My book.

I get out my big notebook and stare at the routine again. With hindsight, it does look like it should be called A Fancy Way to Drown. But that's OK, because I suddenly realize I have a secret weapon.

I WhatsApp the boys.

Meet me at the pool at 7 tomorrow. If you don't feel we've made progress by the time we leave I'll give you last week's £20 back.

I stare at it before pressing *send*. It's missing something. I move the cursor to the front of the message and add:

I'm sorry. You ARE good swimmers. For boys.

The ticks appear, so I know it's sent at least. I wait half an hour, then head back to class. All through afternoon lessons I keep checking my phone, but no one replies. In desperation, at 4.30 p.m. I type:

Those girls can't coach you, they're the competition! Plus, do you really want to flip upside down and choke on your own snot in front of girls you fancy?

Bullet-proof logic, and they seem to agree.

Gabriel
I'm in! It's good to nearly drown, makes you appreciate life ;)

Roman
Go on then.

Pete
Same.

16

I can't wait for the next day to pass so I can show the boys the new routine. So of course, every minute, every second, draaaaags. Mr Peters calls me up to his desk after double English, which I spent scribbling sneakily in my notebook.

"Lou," he says. "I promise, lessons don't drag when you pay attention. I was talking about *Hamlet*, one of the greatest stories in the world. And you were staring at a tree."

"I'm sorry," I say. He has a way of telling me off that makes me feel so guilty. *This* is the sort of emotional blackmail I was trying on Debs and the boys, but I don't have Mr Peters' gift.

He nods at Hannah's empty chair. "Are you missing Banquo's ghost?" he asks.

"I know why that's meant to be funny," I tell him kindly.

"You could've laughed!"

"LOL."

"Go away, Louise. And stop killing time, *participate*!"

If only he could see me now, I think as I set up a flip-chart easel at the swimming pool that evening and sit my big notebook on it. Totes participating.

I arrange my fat marker pens at the bottom and wait for the boys. They arrive a minute later and all stand in front of the notebook. Finally Roman states the obvious.

"It's blank."

"Yes," I say. "I want you to tell me what you like doing and what you're good at, then I will build a routine that you will enjoy. A routine just for *you*, to complement all your skills. And – I'm sorry, that's what I should've said the other day. Not—"

"*I thought you were better swimmers!*" the three of them echo back at me. Oops, I possibly hurt their feelings with that. I hold my hands up in a sorry gesture. But it's worked, they're already softening. They reach for pens and start doodling.

"And," I say, pulling off my jumper because I've

already changed into my swimsuit, "let me give you some ideas."

I dive in from the side and start showing them barrel dives down to the bottom of the pool, and some shapes I can form while I'm down there. When I surface, Pete is shaking his head.

"I can't hold my breath that long!"

I bite back something I want to say but don't dare.

"You could if you quit smoking," Roman tells him sternly.

Bingo. That's the one.

I get them to hop in the pool and try out some easy exercises, then see if we can combine some to make them a little harder.

"Is there something we could do that lets us catch our breath between dives, something on the surface? Surface-work? If that's a Thing?" Gabe asks.

We all shrug at each other. Sure, surface-work: that sounds plausible.

I pretend to think as I pace casually over to my bag and peek at something hidden inside. It's *Swimming for Women and the Infirm*.

Surprisingly helpful if you're trying to teach yourself synchronized swimming and Wikipedia doesn't offer much. But if the boys knew it would hurt their pride, so *ssshhh*.

The session goes so well, we even walk out together. It's like we're friends. (If you glance at us quickly, from a distance.)

"So, shall I work on the routine and we'll meet in two or three days?" I ask slyly.

"Go on, then," says Roman. "And thanks."

"Really, thanks," adds Gabe. I will plan parts of the routine to be easier on him. I don't want to exhaust him.

Pete holds out his hand. "The twenty quid?" he asks.

I look up, shocked. Is he joking? No, he's deadly serious. I think! The moment hangs in the air and I'm so confused. Then Roman slaps him on the shoulder and laughs, and the three of them walk off to Pete's car.

Oh, ha ha.

Gabe turns round to give me a little wave and an apologetic look. Pete's nice, deep down, but there are a lot of layers of Rude Knobhead to chisel away first.

Dad picks me up. I feel guilty now I'm not fired any more, but he doesn't feel that I've abandoned him.

"My employed daughter," he says, ruffling my hair, "is going to buy me chips."

"No she's not!"

"Daddy's so proud!"

"OK, but *small* chips. And no fish!"

17

Weez! Where are you?! I'm fed up. My times aren't getting any faster.

Sorry! I'm here, I'm here. You're just plateauing. Debs taught us that, it happens.

I've cut out carbs but every time they weigh us I get heavier.

You probably weigh more because you're gaining muscle.

Yeah, muscle on my fat bum and gut.

SHUT UP, FATTY.

Han?

All too soon it's the weekend again. This week has been OK. Mr Peters and I have agreed that I will participate in class and he will never make a Shakespeare joke again. He said he had a brilliant one about Bottom, but I was adamant.

English lessons are all right, actually – definitely more interesting than staring out the window. And we've had two swimming training sessions, so it's almost like I have a Thing again! Although it's not my Thing, it's the boys' Thing, I'm just helping them. Still, they need me (and my trusty copy of *Swimming for Women and the Infirm*).

I'm mooching around the house on Saturday morning as usual. Lav is getting ready to go into town. I'm lying on my bed watching her. I wish I had someone to go to the shops with. I could ask Lav, and she might take me with her, but her friends won't like it and I'll feel in the way.

I've already cleaned both cars and my half of the bedroom. Mum and Dad were watching me fearfully as I did this. They kept asking, "What have you done? Why are you sucking up? Have you killed someone?"

It was a relief when I finally put down the hoover and said please could I go to the try-outs for *Britain's Hidden Talent*. It's in the daytime, three weeks today, and I'll be with two boys from school (and one boy who has left school and is in college and smokes... I *don't* say). Yes, of course we'll have an adult with us – Pete's dad.

No, I'm not dating any of the boys, good grief. Lav backed me up on this. They have nothing to worry about there with me.

"*Yet*," said Dad supportively.

Uh-huh. I'm sure I'll be inundated with boys chatting me up aaaany day now. I rolled my eyes, but I know he was just being nice.

They agreed I could go so long as I promised to take my phone with me. (Like I'd leave it behind! I might miss Hannah telling me the calorie content of a peanut.)

My phone vibrates now. Probably another demand from Pete that I change the choreography of the swimming routine so it doesn't mess up his hair. (I'm not even joking.)

It's a WhatsApp message from Gabe saying that he's just realized they'll need some matching swimming gear for the try-outs and is there any chance I'm free today to go to the mall and find some?

There is a big fat wobbly chance I'm free!

I reply immediately: Love to, great idea!

Pete and Roman both reply saying they're busy – of course they are – but I don't care because they make me nervous anyway. I'll have a much nicer time hanging out with Gabe.

"*Muu-uum*... Can I have a lift into town, please?"

"Your dad *just* took Lavender to the mall!"

I go to the top of the stairs; she's standing at the bottom, looking irritable.

"I'm sorry, I only just got asked."

Her eyes narrow. Mum-radar.

"By a *boy*?"

"Yes, but I swear not like that!"

"Oh, really?" She pulls a coat on and grabs her car keys. I take that as a yes and nip downstairs.

"Wait, should I get changed?" I'm just in jeans and a T-shirt.

"If you get changed I'll *know* it is "like that"."

Fine. I won't get changed. I follow her out to the car, reassuring her of the non-romantic nature of my trip.

"Seriously, Mum, I could fit him in my pocket."

"He'll grow."

"So will I!"

We pass Dad driving back from dropping Lav off. Mum points at me with her thumb and gives him an exaggerated eye-roll. I grab the steering wheel so we don't plough into a line of parked cars. Dad's laughing as he drives off.

I wait for Gabe outside the entrance to the shopping mall. I hope we have enough to talk about. We usually chat easily, maybe because he's the only one who's not scared that I fancy him. (For the record, I don't fancy Roman and Pete, but I feel like I *should* and that makes me feel like they think I *do* and ... oh shut up, it's complicated being me.)

But I only know Gabe through swimming training, not as someone to go shopping with. I hope it's not weird, like going to the zoo with your dentist.

I see him before he sees me – he's dressed in khakis and a denim shirt, which are either designer or he's so cool that everything looks designer on him. I tug at the hem of my old T-shirt self-consciously, realizing I probably smell of car cleaning fluid. I'm such a sophisticated lady.

I have a sudden horrible thought: how do we say hello to each other? Kiss on both cheeks? That feels dangerously French. I picture a nightmare scenario in which I grab Gabe firmly by his shoulders and kiss him on both cheeks and afterwards he tells Pete and Roman that I'm a sex pervert.

He's getting closer and I still haven't decided what to do. Argh! He's right in front of me!

"Hi," he says and gives me a quick, friendly hug.

I'm an idiot. I follow him into a cheap sports shop.

"Will Roman and Pete wear something from here?"

"We'll cut the labels out and tell them it's Armani."

We go from shop to shop trying to find something not too expensive but not too cheap, not too baggy but not too clingy. I blush so hard when Gabe holds up some tiny Speedos that I swear I feel the blood leave my feet.

There's like a foot height difference between us – the wrong way, obviously – so I know we must look daft together, but I genuinely don't care. Until we walk past a big group of kids from Lavender and Gabe's year. They start laughing.

"Oi, Gabe, is that your girlfriend?" one guy yells. It's like he's being nasty to me but matey with Gabe. My heart starts beating hard.

"My wife, actually, show some respect," Gabe replies coolly.

There's a confused silence from the group.

"She's massive!" another one calls out and I look to Gabe, wondering how he'll handle this.

"I think the word you're scrabbling for is 'statu-esque'." He smiles back at them like he literally could not care less. And I guess he doesn't, so I don't either. As we walk away, I feel slightly shell-shocked. Judging from the silence behind us, I'm not the only one.

After an hour of intensive swimwear shopping I've touched so much Lycra that my hair has gone static and I keep giving Gabe electric shocks (like a feeble X-Man). We decide to have a coffee and let the electrons dissipate.

We chat about school and I skim over my social status, but...

"That's what I'd heard about you," he says, spooning a mountain of sugar onto his coffee froth with a serious look on his face. It's very sweet.

His face, not the coffee. Though probably both.

"What had you heard about me?" I'm astounded that he'd heard anything at all.

"You don't try to be like everyone else," he shrugs, like it's obvious. "You're not bothered about being popular or dressing cool or having boys fancy you."

It's a compliment; it just *really* doesn't sound like one. I let it pass.

"Who are *your* friends?" I ask, suddenly realizing I don't know much about him.

"People online, with similar illnesses. When I was off school, we'd chat all the time. It's odd being back with people whose biggest problem is growing out a bad fringe."

"Um, your illness. What exactly…?" I trail off, wondering if I'm being nosy.

"It comes and goes," he says. "At its worst it's like having flu *all* the time. You're too exhausted to get out of bed but you can't sleep, and your limbs ache and you can't concentrate on anything. So it's like one long, sleepless night."

"Wow."

"It's OK really."

"Is it?"

"No. I'm just being totally brave and cool about it." He flips his hair back like Roman.

I laugh. And I can see that gang from his year watching us, which makes me laugh even harder. They must be shocked by the sudden improvement in my life. I know I am.

I stop laughing and we sit for a bit in a comfortable silence. Which goes on a little *too* long and it suddenly becomes awkward. Argh! Operation: Make Friends is a minefield – you can't ever relax. I panic and say whatever falls into my head.

"And is there more of you?"

"You mean...?"

"Sorry, I *mean*, have you got siblings?"

"No, just Roman." Gabe smiles as I wave my teaspoon around trying to finish this garbled question. I accidentally flick some milk froth over his shoulder.

"Sorry!"

"That's OK. And you have a sister, don't you?"

"Yeah, she's in your year. Lavender Brown. Dark hair, big eyes. Really, you don't know her?"

I thought *all* the boys in our school knew who she was.

He's still shaking his head.

"She's nice. A bit like your brother." I think about Lav rubbing oil into my hair and I feel bad. "No, that's not fair, she's nicer than Roman."

I suddenly realize how rude that is.

"Not that Roman isn't nice, he's just..." I'm waving my teaspoon again. Gabe holds his napkin up to shield himself from any more flicked froth and I smile and put it down.

Wow, coffee really brings out the truth bombs.

"Maybe," says Gabe, choosing his words carefully, "he feels like he can't be so good-looking and talented for no reason. His life feels smaller than he deserves."

"Poor guy," I say fake-seriously.

"And Pete's always been grumpy."

"But you're not."

"I'm just happy to be out of my pyjamas."

"Congratulations," I say and we cheers coffees. "Now that you are, let's get you into some Lycra."

That sounds sassy in my head, but once I say it … weirdly sexual.

We sit in silence with my strange, accidental flirting hanging in the air.

18

Louise.

I've told you this so many times, I'm worried you've got brain damage. But once again: STAY OUT OF MY HALF OF THE ROOM. I'm trying to live like a dignified human being over here and you are a slob. It's bad enough that I have to look at it, but don't let it spill over into my half. Anything of yours that I find on my side of the room I'll throw out the window.

Lavender.

No kisses.

Lav.

WHY ARE YOU EMAILING ME, I AM THREE FEET AWAY FROM YOU?! I just watched you type that and you just watched me read it. Maybe you couldn't see me properly over the one sock, one notepad and solitary pencil ALL OVER the floor. Aargh, the chaos!! It's cool if you're on your period, but you don't have to advertise it.

Lou.

No kisses.

She is right, my side of the room is a state. It looks like Sports Direct exploded. (God forbid it ever does: that's where I get *all* my clothes.)

I've spent the last three weeks training every lunchtime with the boys, trying to do as much homework as I can between classes, coming home, swallowing dinner, racing out to coach them, then falling into bed as soon as I get in. I am tired.com/pooped.

You know when you walk into a room and you can't remember what you went in for?

I did that today, in the toilet.

The night before the try-outs we have our usual training session. I've never seen the boys this nervous. Afterwards we stand around the pool, talking through the routine one more time. We only stop when I get a stern text from my dad telling me he's been sitting in the car park for half an hour and if I don't come out he's going to come in and get me.

I AM WEARING MY SHORTS PYJAMAS WITH THE VERY SHORT SHORTS, his message ends. I run to the car.

Dad says I'm too late for dinner so I'll have to go to bed hungry. I don't believe him for a second and we get home to a lasagne in the oven. I hope he never moves out. Though I don't know how Mum would feel about that. Surely *one* day she'll have a successful date and end up with a boyfriend?

Heading up to bed full of anxiety and pasta, I get a sudden urge to tell Hannah how I'm feeling. But every time we talk these days she's just stressing about her training and her fitness and doesn't seem interested in me. So, *fine*.

Her last text was about how all the other girls at the camp have a thigh gap, and do I have one?

Yes, I reply. If I stick my bum out like a constipated duck.

I'd give my right leg for a thigh gap.

If you lose a leg you'll have all the thigh gap you want!

No reply.

The morning of the try-outs dawns bright and clear. Possibly. I wouldn't know, I don't wake up at dawn – I'm not a farmer.

My alarm goes off at 5 a.m., which is still *horrendous*, and Lav has a slurred half-asleep tantrum at me.

I try to get ready without waking anyone else up but the ancient plumbing in our house has other ideas. By the time it's belched out my hot water for a shower and flushed the toilet with a load of grumbling complaints, everyone is awake. They're all staggering and yawning, bumping into each other and getting tangled in their dressing gowns. No one in this family functions well in the mornings.

I sit at the bottom of the stairs waiting for the boys to arrive. Pete said his dad would come by in the pick-up truck at 5.30 a.m. and can I *please* stop questioning him about how he's getting the tank to the studio.

"NO!!" I shout to Mum. "I am *not* eating my packed lunch already!" Jeez, some people.

Oooh, cheese and pickle.

Lav comes and sits two steps behind me.

"Y'ellooo?" I greet her through a mouthful of cheese.

"Are you going like that?" she asks.

"Lav, I'm about to queue in the rain for a million hours then assemble a ... sort of tank. I don't think it's a dressy day."

"No, that's what I *mean*!" She jumps up again and heads upstairs. "Haven't you ever queued for a gig?" she yells over her shoulder. She comes back with a sleeping bag in her arms and piles of jumpers. "You will freeze your bum off," she informs me, "then you will bore it off."

"So either way," I conclude, "I'm coming home without my bottom. The one part of my body that looks vaguely normal. That's a real shame."

I take the sleeping bag off her and start putting one of the jumpers on, when there's a terrifyingly loud hoot from outside.

Lav and I freeze. You know when you hear a dog and just *know* from its bark that it's a monster? Lav opens the front door and we peer out. There, blocking the whole road, is the biggest truck I've ever seen in my (admittedly, not truck-filled) life.

It looks like the sort of thing you'd use to move a circus. Pete, Roman, Gabe and a man in a baseball cap are all sitting in the front. Gabe gives me a queenly wave out of the window. The man in the baseball cap looks like he's tempted to stick him in the back with the tank.

"So. I guess that's my ride," I say.

"Please be careful!" Mum calls down. She's peering out of an upstairs window.

As if I've got control over anything that happens today! I shoulder my sleeping bag and stagger out into the street.

Our neighbours are starting to open their front doors to stare at this monstrosity in their road. I give them all a little wave, feeling like a celebrity.

The truck door opens three feet above my head and I look at it helplessly. I've never had to jump *up* into a vehicle before.

This must be how short people live.

Gabe reaches down for my stuff and then Roman reaches past him and pulls me up into the cab, where the boys are already squashed together. I land on the springy seat. It smells like an ashtray in here, and as Pete's dad nods at me, then taps a cigarette delicately on to the floor, I see why.

"Hello, Mr..." I say. Then realize I don't actually know Pete's last name, so it sounds like I just called his dad "mister". He grips his cigarette between his teeth and simply says, "Pete," while throwing the mega-truck into reverse.

Pete's dad is called *Pete*?

Who gives their kid their own name and doesn't think that might get confusing when yelled around the house? You only give your child the same name as you if you're royalty or you don't plan on living with them.

Like I can talk – my parents are divorced and you know the saying: People in glass houses ... go to slightly smaller glass houses every other weekend to see their dad.

I sit back gingerly. The seat is sticky, but it's probably for the best as there are no seatbelts. Gabe and I make big eyes at each other: half *This is fun!* and half *Maybe today we'll die!*

Pete's dad slams on the brakes and we all lurch forward. Then he accelerates for about three inches and slams on the brakes again before going into reverse. We do this maybe ten times. It gets nauseating pretty quickly.

My family have now all congregated at the front door and I wave at them with a big smile on my face. I might as well.

If this is the last time they ever see me, let's give them a happy memory.

Gabe peeks around me and joins in. Mum makes a

face like a ventriloquist's dummy and says something out of the corner of her mouth to Lav.

He's nice-looking.

Lav makes the same face. *Short, though.*

Dad weighs in, with *growth spurt* mouthed nice and clearly. I can see him wrestling with a breeze up his dressing gown that threatens to embarrass us all. Thanks, family! And there I was thinking, He-ey, it's almost 6 a.m. and my ears haven't burnt with shame once today.

Roman leans forward to give a friendly nod to my family, then Pete's dad reverses into our neighbour's front garden and takes that pesky bird bath off their hands. Roman leans back out of sight.

Pete murmurs something in his ear.

"Oh, go on," I say. They turn to look at me.

"What?"

I sigh. "I know exactly what you're thinking, just say it."

Roman says, "Your sister is gorgeous," at the exact same moment as Gabe says, "Your dad *does* have great legs for his age... Oh wait, no, not that?" We all laugh, even Pete.

I feel a bit bad laughing with my new friends *at* my

family, but it's not mean and I secretly feel very happy.

Not friends. Did I say friends? I meant Sports Colleagues.

"Sooo…" I say, to fill the silence as we jerk backwards and forwards on our forty-one-point turn. "What's your surname, Pete?"

"Who's asking?" grunts his dad, fixing me with a stare. He couldn't be dodgier if he had a bag marked "swag" over one shoulder.

I can't believe he works at the aquarium – I wouldn't trust him with a fish finger.

"So, the tank, is it…" I wait for someone to leap in and finish my question. But Roman and Gabe give me tiny shrugs – obviously they've no idea about fish tanks either – so I plough on alone. "Is it, like, flat-pack, or…?"

Pete's dad stares at me as if I've said something stupid, but I'm cool with not knowing anything about fish tanks. He chews his soggy cigarette over to the corner of his mouth and says, "I dismantled it to get it out the window. Gorra assemble it the other end."

Get it out the window? I concentrate on breathing in through my nose and out through my mouth and try not to get stressed. While I'm doing that, Pete's dad picks up a screwdriver and hands it to me.

It's a sort of friendly gesture, like: *You and me, pal, we can build this huge, criminal tank.*

Gabriel leans over and we scrutinize it together with exaggerated care as if it's a dug-up dinosaur bone. I'm about to get the giggles so I signal him to stop. Pete's dad seems a bit unpredictable. Let's not poke the beast.

Driving in the mega-truck is *so* exciting. We're kings of the road! (Kings in the old-fashioned sense, where you slaughter people left, right and centre.) Roman, Pete, Gabe and I spend most of the journey ducking down to look in the wing mirrors, praying that the cyclist we just drove past is still upright. Thankfully they all are, but I don't think I've ever seen so many rude gestures in my life.

I'm wishing someone from school could see me with the guys, but – just my luck – we're too high up to be seen. Maybe I could take an "accidental" selfie...

19

Weezy, I'm so busy here, it's manic. I feel like I
barely have time to think. I just swim, swim, swim
and I'm always nervous! Mum's nagging me and
I haven't so much as SEEN a carb in days. I miss
them, and you. Do you miss me?

Hxxxxxxxx

I'm trying to text Han back, but the truck's bouncy
suspension makes me feel sick. I'll tell her the good news
when we get through the try-outs. Eventually the mega-
truck pulls up outside a massive modern building. It's
made almost entirely of windows. Must be a nightmare
to clean, I tut to myself, sounding like Dad.

There's a queue of hundreds of people shelter-
ing under umbrellas and here's us pulling up in the

mega-truck like total bosses. I have never felt more cool. I'm nearest to the window so I roll it down and lean out super-casually, like I own the truck. Mmm-hmm, yes, it's a left-hand drive and I've got a young face.

I've never seen the appeal in smoking, but right now I'd love to fling a cigarette out of the window with a world-weary gesture, like: *Hey, it's just another TV gig.*

Pete Senior opens his window, flicks his soggy cigarette out with a world-weary gesture ... and follows it with a gob of spit.

Less TV Star, more Loitering Outside William Hill.

I eye up the posters for upcoming gigs. I've never been to a gig here (or anywhere else, if I'm honest) but Lav's been to a couple with her mates.

"Oh, I've been here," says Roman. "I came for a football sticker swap meet years ago. They made us queue outside in the rain for three hours."

"That's ridiculous!" I say.

"Nah, we only stayed forty minutes, did all our swaps in the queue and by the time they opened the doors we'd gone."

"All right," wheezes Pete's dad, "let's park up." He puts the handbrake on and swings himself out of the cab. Really? Here?

We clamber down and join him. It looks as if we've just parked in the middle of a square – you know, the sort of place where people eat sandwiches, drink a coffee with friends and *don't* park trucks?

"You lot go get in the queue," says Pete's dad, wrestling with the doors at the back. "I'll unload."

"Should we help?" Roman asks Pete.

"Heavy work, lads," Pete Senior sniffs.

"Don't bother offering," Pete tells him, walking away. "When my dad looks at me he just sees a seven-year-old in a tutu."

Pete did *ballet* as a kid? Roman sniggers. I don't think I was meant to hear that. I hang back so he doesn't realize I did.

"Shut up, Ro. You never heard of Billy Elliot?"

I want to join in but I still don't feel like one of them so I don't risk it.

At the front of the queue is a massive opening into a huge warehouse-like area.

You could park a plane in there and lose it when you came back from your shopping.

We peer in. It's full of cameras, and men with walkie-talkies, and young women with clipboards, and big black floor-to-ceiling curtains partitioning off different sections. I'm nervous at the thought of being in the middle of that madness.

But that won't be for a while, because first we have to queue.

The line is about five deep; the people at the front are sprawled on the floor as if part of a disastrous sleepover. They're giving off a nasty whiff – sports sock full of egg – and look mad around the eyes.

We walk along the queue, looking – hoping – for the end of it. We walk and we walk, and the queue just keeps on … *being*. After we follow it around the building for over five minutes, it no longer looks like a queue, more like the population of a medium-sized country with a whimsical sense of humour said, "Hey guys, let's stand in a sausage shape today!"

There are a lot of dogs in dresses. This is going to be a day I'll never forget. (Which can be a good thing or a bad thing. I'll also never forget the day I had chicken pox and got a scab up my nose.)

A ferret wearing a tiny cowboy hat darts at Gabe's ankle, teeth bared.

"Anastasia, no!"

Its owner, a skinny teenager with flesh tunnels in each ear, scolds the ferret and scoops it up.

By now we're at the end of the queue. I think Gabe would rather be further away from the ferret.

"Who calls a ferret Anastasia?" wonders Roman.

"The sort of person who dresses it up in a cowboy hat," Gabe replies.

Pete looks worried. "I hope there are some normal people here, and we're not just auditioning for a freak show."

Now he worries about that?

"Underwater synchronized dancing probably fits right in," mutters Roman, who seems to be losing his nerve. I have to do something.

I give a little peep on my whistle and they all look at me.

"Let's sit and wait and stay focused," I tell them with a confidence that I do not feel. Thankfully no one argues back.

I pull on another jumper and wriggle into my sleeping bag. After a few minutes of squirming I finally slide into a comfy position. I look up to see all the boys watching me.

"Have you never queued for a gig?"

We sit there *for ever*. OK, forty minutes, but that's a really long time to sit on the ground. The queue keeps moving forward tiny bit by tiny bit, which is such a pain in the butt – literally – cos I'm shuffling along on it every thirty seconds to keep up.

Eventually the boys take pity on me and drag me behind them like a bag of rubbish.

I will really need to wash my hair tonight, I think as I feel it scrape along the tarmac.

More and more people join the queue behind us, so at least we feel like we're ahead of *someone*. Then I see an unwelcome sight: an upside-down view of Debs, Cammie, Melia, Nicole and Amanda walking past us. Cammie stops when she sees Pete. I sit up and knock a sweet wrapper out of my hair.

Debs notices that her team has stopped and comes back to see what's happening. "Oh, hello," she says, vaguely drifting her eyes over everyone as if she doesn't really remember us. Cheers, ex-favourite teacher. She recognizes the boys and I see her putting two and two together. So *that's* what we were doing at the pool.

"Are you going to queue?" I ask.

"No," she says. The girls smile a little, like: *Oh how lol, but I can't laugh or I'd crack my make-up.*

"We got through weeks ago," says Debs smoothly. "We're here to do interviews, dress rehearsal with our bespoke swimming pool … you know."

I nod, but I don't know, especially the word "bespoke".

I hope it means "full of snakes".

"Uh-huh," says Gabe. (*Love* Gabe, I'm so glad he's picked up on the tone here. The other two are just dribbling over the girls. Please *focus*, team.)

"Yah, we've got a free-standing swimming pool too. Ours is industrial, though, higher build-quality – well, you know…" he says, having an elaborate stretch and yawn to show how very unbothered he is.

I'm quietly googling *bespoke* on my phone inside my sleeping bag so Debs can't see. Oh, it just means someone made it for them. Well, someone *is* making our pool for us, *actually*, so…

"Oi!!" comes a yell from behind.

Great timing, Pete Senior.

"Oi!!!" he says again, clearly keen for the whole queue to hear. "I've got yer fish tank set up!"

20

At the words "fish tank" I can see everyone in the queue starting to giggle and look around. There are people who put hats on their ferrets and dresses on their dogs and they are laughing at *us*.

"Thanks, Dad!" yells Pete, leaping to his feet. Then he sees the tank and his face droops. I haul myself up using Gabe as a crutch, stumble over a few magazines and shuffle over to stand next to Pete. We stare together.

Well. If one were to scrabble around for a nice thing to say (and let's be nice, why not?), it looks a bit like modern art. It lurches and bulges wonkily at the sides. I can't imagine it holding a small mouse, let alone gallons of water. And it's really small – the swimming routine is going to involve a lot more cuddling than I'd choreographed.

Also, *how* are we going to move it into the studio? Already a traffic warden is eyeing it up and reaching for his notebook.

"We won't keep you," I say crisply to Debs and her team. They drift off with a couple of pitying backwards glances and sniggers.

"Stay here," says Pete to me, wearily. "Hold our place." Happy to! His dad was tetchy when I asked him his surname, imagine how moody he'll be when questioned about his crazy fish bowl. I watch the three boys slope away towards the wobbly upside-down greenhouse in the middle of the pedestrianized zone.

My stomach is churning with cheese, pickle and worry. I fiddle with my whistle. Usually that bolsters my confidence, but right now I feel out of my depth. I think about calling home, but I've got no bars.

Pete, Roman and Gabe finish talking with Pete Senior and walk back to me with the faces of men who have seen their own doom and know there is nothing left to do but face it with dignity.

"Good news?" I say brightly.

Gabe looks at Pete, who says nothing. Gabe fills me in. "We have no idea how we can move it from out here to in there. *And*, that tank is so small that if we attempt the triple dive someone's going to end up pregnant. It can't be me because I need to focus on my education."

I sink deep inside my sleeping bag. All this hard work for nothing! After a few seconds I poke my head back out to see what's going on. They've fallen silent. Roman and Gabriel are staring at Pete in utter astonishment.

"What?" I demand, pushing my hair out of my face. "What have I missed?"

"Pete just apologized," whispers Roman.

"Do it again," says Gabriel incredulously.

"Oh, shut up!" snaps Pete. "I'm sorry, OK? I really thought my dad would come through for me."

"To be fair..." I say slowly.

"Oh seriously, Lou, can you not?" interrupts Pete.

How is *everyone* allowed to make fun of him except me?

"I wasn't going to!" I protest. "I was going to say that he got a gigantic truck across town, carrying a quite big and –" I hiss this bit – "*stolen* fish tank in it *and* he managed to put it together, sort of. Your dad did all that because he loves you, and it's still amazing..." I trail off, suddenly becoming shy again.

Pete's dad ambles up.

"No good, then?"

We hesitate.

"It's brilliant, Dad, thanks," lies Pete and hugs his dad, who gives him a surprisingly comfortable hug back.

"Thanks, Pete!" we all say with big fake smiles.

"Good," says his dad. "Call me when you need me, I'll be in the pub."

"Aaahh," says Gabe as we watch Pete Senior wander off. "I love to hear those words from the man who's driving me home in a ten-ton truck."

There's a shrieking, scratching noise behind us and we turn around just in time to see the tank collapse in on itself. A raggedy cheer and round of applause rise up from the queue.

So it's come to this: Plan B, as in Bloody Stupid.

I wriggle out of my sleeping bag and divest myself of a couple of jumpers. I'm walking to my doom and I don't want to look like a laundry basket that sprouted legs. I've been formulating a desperate idea for the past ten minutes, which I really hoped I wouldn't have to put into action. I head towards the TV cameras at the front of the queue.

I see Debs from the back, she's standing just inside the entrance to the aircraft hangar. She's leaning on one leg slightly, hand on hip. Even when she's relaxed Debs always looks ready to pounce and kill. Which doesn't help right now.

"Debs?" I say. She doesn't turn around. She's watching her girls give an interview to two smooth-faced men holding microphones.

"COACH!" I yell and she wheels round. Instinct.

"Can I talk to you?" I ask.

"Not now." She turns back, dismissing me. Hannah would do this so much better than me, but she's not here. I grab hold of my inner Hannah and take a deep breath.

"Durbs!" I announce in a reedy shout.

Oops: spit bubble in my throat. *Ahem*.

"Debs!" I shout less froggily. "I'm sorry I didn't swim fast enough at the Olympic time trials, I'm sorry that after all your coaching and hard work I just wasn't good enough! I'm a failure!" The camera moves over to me.

"But now I've coached a team of swimmers for this show and it's helping me feel confident again! I just want a chance to show what we can do and make my gran proud. My gran who ... died." I shield my eyes so I don't cry (very little risk of that tbh, both my grans are fine). The crowd around me murmurs sympathetically. I've seen this show, I know how it works. I lift my face out of my hands and do Big Eyes at Debs.

"So please, Debs, can we borrow your ... bespoke pool?" The world goes very quiet as I stare at her.

Debs has a peculiar look on her face and I realize she doesn't know what to *feel*, let alone fake. I really have got her on her weakest area here. Genius, Lou! And only a little bit humiliating for me – but no worse than having tampons flicked at your head.

"That's a beautiful story," says one of the presenters, putting an arm around each of us. From the look on Debs' face I'd be surprised if he gets that back in one piece.

"Great back story. I *know* we can't wait to see these two former teammates become rivals today." He's not really talking to us, he's twinkling at the camera. Debs looks homicidal, so I say, "Thanks, coach!" and run off.

"Hey!" A man with a walkie-talkie gestures to me. I hesitate, bouncing on the balls of my feet. "The pool will be here. Come and find us when you're a hundred away from the head of the queue, OK?"

I nod and run off to tell the boys.

21

My team are so pleased with me that they spend a tenner on snacks from the local petrol station and shower me in crisps. An hour later, the crisps are all gone and my hair feels salty, but I feel happy. This audition might actually happen. I make the boys stretch so their muscles don't stiffen up. They protest that they look stupid.

I nod at a woman dressed as a cow. This is not the place for shy people: get stretchy.

Roman keeps running to the front of the queue to count back and see how far away we are from the front. Finally he sprints back, shouting, "Ninety-eight!"

"OK, people, this is go, go, go!!" I say, sounding a bit like Debs. We sprint to the entrance. I'm blinking in the unfamiliar darkness when a blank-faced security man puts his hand on my chest.

"Sorry, sir…"

I take out my hairclip and my hair tumbles down.

He takes his hand off my chest *very* quickly and begins apologizing. I nip past him and find my walkie-talkie guy, who is standing on top of a big podium shouting and pointing at things. Everyone's very busy here, in a sort of "behold my busyness, marvel at my loud efficiency!" kinda way.

"Excuse me!" I shout up at him, my voice sounding all weedy in the aircraft hangar but aware that the security guard will soon be hot on my heels.

"It's me, swimming pool girl? Can we have a look at the pool we're borrowing, please?" He nods at me and whispers something stern to his wrist. I hope he's got a microphone in there. Our last pool-provider was a bit mad, we need this one to be sane.

"OK," he says, stepping down from the podium and heading towards us. He's listening to something in his earpiece and talking to us but looking three feet above our heads.

"They're just finishing up in there, the girls were doing a demo for the cameras." He jerks his head towards a big black curtain behind him. I'm desperate to see Debs' routine and I step forward without thinking. Wrist Man puts a hand up to stop me.

I can hear splashing and bare feet padding around in there, some murmured thank yous, then silence. Wrist Man peers around the curtain and nods at us to go through, holding it open for us. Gabe plucks at my arm in excitement, I pluck his back, painfully hard, and we do *Eeee!* faces at each other. We step through the curtain and stop, dazzled by the bright studio lights.

The pool is a huge, free-standing circle, about twelve feet high. It dwarfs us and it takes me a few seconds to walk all the way around it, running my fingers admiringly along its sides.

All the way along … its … sides.

The sides are made of black plastic. I can't see into the pool. Of course, because they're doing normal synchronized swimming. I'm an idiot.

I keep walking until I bump into the boys. Pete is resting his forehead on the side, looking suddenly very tired.

"You can't see in," he says, stating the obvious. Gabe picks at one of the edges.

"It won't come off," he adds.

Roman thumps his head a few times against the side of the pool.

Debs appears. "Stop that. It's bespoke."

We walk back outside in silence, past Wrist Man and the presenters, who look confused about the kids who skipped into the studio and trudged out minutes later, all hope gone. Once we're outside we turn left as if to rejoin the queue, then we realize there's no point.

"You didn't even *see* the pool?" Pete asks me.

"No!" I say. "I couldn't, cos it was backstage. I didn't even think. I … I just thought I'd fixed everything," I trail off miserably.

"Never mind," says Roman, but he doesn't sound at all like he means it.

We head towards Pete's dad's truck. It seems the only thing to do. Mum calls as we walk. I tell her what happened in a half-whisper. Right now I feel like Pete and Roman are having to stop themselves from yelling at me. This isn't fair. I did my best. Gabe puts a comforting arm around my shoulders. Luckily I'm stooped with sadness or he would have struggled to reach.

Mum rings off. Just as I'm thinking, "Never mind, in a couple of hours I'll be in bed eating cheese on toast," I spot that the mega-truck has been clamped.

Then I see Pete Senior weaving towards us with the snooty air of a drunk person who's trying to hide it and

I'm grateful that it has. Dad does this at Christmas: "Ah am *shimply* overwhelmed by all the festivitivitivi – turkey."

"Oh, balls," says Pete Senior, giving the clamp a half-hearted kick. He takes it very well, I must say, but I guess if you don't plan ahead you're less fussed when things go wrong.

We stand around the collapsed fish tank while Pete's dad makes a series of phone calls to friends. We don't stand too close in case it collapses further – and because a bored queue of hopeful *BHT* contestants are taking selfies in front of it. They're all obviously going to end up online and I don't want to be tagged.

Not that I'm on Facebook. It's one thing to not have *loads* of friends but there's no need to flaunt it publicly.

Pete's dad fetches us coffee from the petrol station. I go to drink mine and it tastes like licking a battery. This is not going to help my stomach ache, but it makes me feel so adult. Finally, three cars turn up. The drivers all nod at Pete, then go into a huddled chat with his dad. They take a couple of shards of glass each and wedge them in the backs of their cars.

It's quite impressive, like ants transporting a leaf.

A leaf that will slice your head off if you brake too

suddenly. I'm glad we're not travelling with them.

Hang on: how *are* we getting home? We look at each other as the last car leaves, and realize, yup, our TV dreams have gone so badly wrong that we arrived in a mega-truck but are leaving by bus. Hello, Hollywood!

Hollywood Bowl, just off the A-road, that's my stop.

We ride the bus in dejected silence, I'm WhatsApping Lav. As I type, something rubs against my chest. It's my whistle tucked under my T-shirt. I hold it for comfort.

"OK," I say suddenly. "This wasn't our last chance. There is one more public try-out. It's next week and we will be ready. We have one week to *find a tank*. We're ready, the routine is ready. We can do this."

The boys look doubtful, as do the people around us on the bus. So I pull out my whistle and give it a quiet but encouraging peep.

"We *can*!" I repeat.

"Yeah," nods Gabriel. "OK."

"Yeah," says Roman, with the hint of a smile.

"Yes!" says a man sitting behind me, caught up in the mood of the moment. (He is *not* joining the team.)

After a pause, Pete shoots me his first smile since he saw Debs' bloody *bespoke* pool.

One week: we can do this. I hold tight to my whistle. I am a coach and this is my team.

22

Lou

Oh god Lav, DISASTER at BHT. I don't know where to begin.

Lav

I've got the headlines.

Lou

How do you know already??

Lav

Twitter.

Lou

AAARRRGGH!!! **Kills self**

Lav

No no it's OK, it's not that bad I swear.

Lou

Really? HOW?!

Lav

Most people are misspelling your name.

Lou

LOU...?

Lav

People are idiots.

Lou

Are they misspelling Roman, Gabe or Pete?

Lav

No.

Lou

I feel sick.

Lav

This will all blow over. Remember when that sixth former wet herself in assembly?

Lou

No.

Lav

Exactly.

No wonder Roman and Pete were so grumpy. They have cool to lose, unlike me. Still, this whole thing is not my responsibility. I'm younger than them and they treat me like their mum *and* a servant.

But I'm not going to get resentful about it: I've done enough feeling sorry for myself this summer. We just have to find a tank. (However many times I say that, it still sounds ridiculous.)

That night I go to bed early, tired out after the 5 a.m. start and the public humiliation. Thankfully, my parents didn't make me go through it all again when I got in. Dad just handed me a giant Aero.

I lie in bed feeling bizarrely optimistic despite everything. At least I'm not dealing with this alone.

I wish I could talk to Hannah about it. Lav isn't the same – she knows more than me, so it feels more like advice than conversation. Right on cue she addresses me from the opposite bed. No "Are you awake?" or any of that polite nonsense. Lav has decided it's chat o'clock, so Chat Hats on and off we go. She looks up from her phone, musing.

"The trouble with boys," she says seriously, "is that they will invariably try and kiss you."

I can't help it; I start laughing.

"Yes, Lavender," I reply, "that is my problem with boys, they are always trying to kiss me. I am like bread in a duck pond. Also I wish they would stop writing me love songs. It gets tedious."

There is a thoughtful silence.

"Are you being sarcastic?"

"*Yes!* Yes, of course I'm being sarcastic. Good *grief*, Lavender."

"You're so pretty," she says.

"Don't," I say firmly. "Even to be nice. I am huge. My hair is mad. I am ripped with muscles. *I* would be scared to meet me down a dark alleyway."

"You're like one of those androgynous catwalk models!" she protests.

"That's as may be, but this is not a catwalk in Milan. This is a suburban town where men yell out of cars to ask if I've escaped from a zoo."

"I'm going to give you a makeover," she says firmly. I sigh.

Lavender thinks that makeovers are the answer to all humanity's problems. If you dropped her into a war zone she'd start shaping everyone's eyebrows.

I feel my eyebrows. They are quite bad, actually, like slugs covered in dog hair. I try to comb them into roughly the right direction with my fingernails.

"Just leave it, Lav," I say quietly into the darkness. I say I don't care, but I guess I do because I feel my throat grow hot and tight.

"Come here," she says, leaping out of bed and grabbing me by the arm. It is *so* scary when someone light-footed does that in the dark. She leads me out of our room and we feel our way along the hallway into Mum's room, where she's trying to sleep.

"Mum," says Lav, "isn't Lou pretty?" Mum pushes her eye mask up and stares at us groggily.

"She's going to be," she finally answers.

"When?" I demand.

"Soon."

Uh-huh. I'd like a more specific time frame on that, tbh. I don't want to die just as I get pretty with everyone at my funeral saying, "Such a shame, she finally grew into that nose."

Lav flops down next to Mum and I crawl in the other side. Mum groans but throws the duvet over both of us.

"You're too big for this," she tuts.

"Mum, don't fat-shame."

"Shut up, Lavender," she mumbles.

We lie still for a bit.

"Mum?" I whisper.

"Yes," she whispers back.

"Is Dad OK?"

I know Lav is listening too.

"He will be."

"Are you guys going to get back together?"

"No, he'll find a pretty redhead and they'll have lots of little sheds together."

"*Mum.*"

"Go to sleep."

23

08:30

Great performance yesterday, guys, not a single weak link. This is the strongest team I've ever coached. A few of you will be following Hannah soon!

Debs

08:31

Thanks Debs!

Nic x

08:33

Thanks Debs! Btw Lou is still on this group thread, can we take her off it? ;)

Cammie xxxxxx

Apparently creativity works best within constraints. I read that somewhere. I have to remind myself of this on Monday when we find that Debs has booked out the swimming pool every evening this week and we have nowhere to practise. I *knew* she'd do something like this.

The boys don't always manage the final lift where Gabe is raised out of the water with Pete and Roman holding a foot each. The *idea* is that he balances there, leaning forward in a controlled pose before the boys throw him up into a high, graceful somersault.

Half the time they perform this perfectly, the rest of the time they slap him into the pool with a loud belly flop. Gabe says not to worry, he never wanted kids anyway.

It took me ages to get that joke.

My little emotional blackmail trick at the try-outs has backfired and Debs is now watching me like a hawk in hotpants. The situation is so desperate that Ro actually *talks to me in public*. Alert the media.

We're standing next to the vending machine at break and he stares intently at the chocolate throughout the conversation so no one will think he's talking to the big muscly weirdo two years below him.

"I don't know where else we can go, I'm sorry!" I tell him for the thousandth time.

"Well, *think*," he says impatiently. "This is your job."

"No, *actually*," I tell him, "my job was helping you put together a routine without you all drowning. I have done that and I have worked *so* hard on this … so … don't tread on me."

You go, girl! I'm glad I had the guts to say that. Pete and Roman can get so focused on what they want that they don't care about anything or anyone else.

If only you could put Gabe's sensitive head on top of one of their bodies. Mmmm. Frankensteinboy.

I get a WhatsApp message from Pete in maths, where for once I'm being left alone in my own seat. Our maths teacher *loves* making us pair off to do maths exercises together. Why? Pairing off doesn't make maths more fun, like: *We're Good Cop, Bad Cop! We're mavericks but we get results!* All that ever happens is that no one wants to be my partner, so I have to pair up with the teacher. Who doesn't help me because SHE IS THE MATHS TEACHER AND KNOWS THE ANSWERS.

The WhatsApp says: Outside the pool at 9 tonight. Wear dark clothes.

Srsly? If Mum knew a boy had sent me such a dodgy text she'd be straight down the police station! Although the thought of Roman – or Pete – thinking of me That Way is hilaire. I'm not sure either of them *realize* I'm a girl. I message back.

I'll bring weapons, you sort alibis.

Roman
Cool

Pete
K

Gabriel
Oh man I am NOT going back to prison.

Two people in this team are doing all the heavy lifting funny-wise.

I'm just putting my phone back in my pocket when it buzzes with a new email from Hannah. I skim-read with one eye on the teacher. She's starting to worry me – she sounds more and more stressed. I hope her parents aren't giving her a hard time, or that the camp isn't picking up where they leave off. The last thing she needs is to be tag-team pressurized.

"*Lou-eeze!*" snaps Ms Kearney.

"Four!" I call out. (Yell a number, it's always worth a try.) From the look on her face it was wrong. And from the silence in the room it must have been quite funny. If I say something embarrassing, it's like someone's detonated a LOL bomb in the classroom, but funny gets nothing.

Lav is so right. They're not friends I haven't made yet, it's just bad luck they were born near me. I moodily doodle a fish tank on my maths book. I put Cammie in it and add a shark, and leave them to it.

24

Weez, are you there? I've had such a bad day. My
times have started getting worse. I feel really slug-
gish. Plus I'm homesick and eating to feel better,
but that's the LAST thing I should do. Told Mum
I want to come home. She said she won't let me
make a mistake I'll regret. So I'm stuck here. Come
bust me out?! Joking not joking.

Hx

That evening I eat dinner thinking about Hannah
and wondering if I should talk to my parents about her.
Or maybe Lav, or Mr Peters? Debs? No way, not Debs.

I feel like showing Hannah's emails to anyone would
be disloyal. I reply and tell her to stay calm, she's probably just having an off week (or month... I *don't* add).

I send her some photos of us camping, and a few badly stuffed animals. If they don't make her smile, she's in real trouble.

It's only when the clock strikes seven that I remember I have a more immediate problem. I haven't asked Mum and Dad for permission to go out tonight. How can I?

"Muu-uum, Daa-aad, can I go out late at night with three boys you don't know? I also suspect we're off to do something dodgy. Don't wait up! And has anyone got money for vodka?"

It's time to call in some favours. I corner Lav as we're washing up after dinner and tell her the problem.

"Wow." She pauses mid-scrub. "That almost sounds cool. Who are you and what have you done with Lou?"

"Ha ha," I say. "But help me. You've sneaked out loads of times to meet boys – how do you do it?"

"Not 'loads' of times!" she protests.

"Lav, I used to see you *walk past* my window on the flat roof. I didn't think Santa Claus had lost weight."

"Ah, was that when we had our own bedrooms?"

"Oh yes. The glory days. Over now."

"You tell them you feel ill and need to go to bed. You say your tummy and back hurt…" She winks at me.

I wink back.

She winks again.

"Lav, why are we winking?"

"Oh for goodness' sake. If I have to spell it out... When's your period due?"

"Er ... the futuuure?"

"Seriously, you haven't started yet?"

"I'm all muscly and my BMI is a bit ... and shut up, yeah? Don't make me self-conscious about it!"

"I just thought you were dealing with it without any fuss."

"Oh no, when it happens I will make a fuss. Now go back to the winking."

"OK, when you say your tummy and back hurt, Dad hears period alarm bells and he'll give you a hot water bottle and leave you alone."

"Brilliant!"

"Yes, *but*, Mum will become more interested in you and hover around. There's a book called *Blossoming into a Woman* that is literally the worst book ever written and she'll want to read it with you. However, she's going out tonight, so the plan is solid."

"What time is she heading out?"

"Eight forty-five."

"I've got to meet them at nine."

"So you're blossoming at eight forty-six, sharp."

It's now 8.50 p.m. and Mum *still* hasn't gone out. She's sitting on the sofa all dressed up, but she seems pretty happy watching TV with Dad. They're shouting insults at *Question Time* and laughing till they snort.

Lav and I sit stony-faced, watching them. Every time they glance in our direction we slap big smiles on our faces, like: *Good one!! David Cameron, eh?* (No idea. I have too many problems in my life to care about national ones.) *Finally* at 9 p.m. Mum kisses all of us and heads out – to meet Dan, whoever he is. Apparently he's "in stocks". Sounds like a man from the Middle Ages being pelted with rotten veg. Best of luck, Mum.

The moment the front door slams I look at Lav. She shakes her head. We wait, and there's the familiar sound of Mum's car starting up and driving off.

Lav nods. Operation: Blossom is a go.

"Ooh," I say, "my stomach hurts."

"Oh dear," says Dad, eyes on the TV.

"And my back," I add. "And I feel sort of emotional."

Lav shoots me daggers. Too much.

Dad gives me his full attention now. "Would you like a hot water bottle?"

"I'll get it," Lav says, giving him A Look. "Maybe Lou should have an early night."

"OK," I say, like: *If you think I should.*

"Feel better, Goldfish!" Dad calls as we shuffle upstairs slowly.

"That was awful, just in case you were wondering," Lav hisses, poking me in the back as she follows me up.

"Sorry, Lav, I've never rebelled before."

We change pace the moment we reach the bedroom. It's 9.03 p.m. and it takes me at least ten minutes to run to the swimming pool. *Aargh!*

I shake off my dressing gown. Underneath it I'm dressed like a mime, head to toe in black. Quite a nice outfit, actually, as Lav supplied most of it.

I put one foot out of the window, ready to drop gently onto the flat roof and sneak off over the garage and down via the water butt as instructed. *Without* snagging the clothes on anything. Crucial instruction. Lav says if I rip her clothes I should keep running, never look back and live life on the run. It's a bit tempting given how much I hate school.

I turn back, and Lav is expertly folding clothes and pillows to stuff under the duvet. She glances up at me.

"Just in case he comes up. I'll stay here now and tell

him you're asleep. Now hurry, you're late. Go make a cool evening uncool."

I drop gently onto the roof and run over the garage like a cartoon burglar, with pointed toes and fingers. Hee hee, this is *fun*! When I get to the edge, I sit down and hook my legs over the side, feeling for the water butt with one foot. I have to be careful: the top is slimy with mildew. I reach down further and further but still can't feel it. I've got the longest legs of anyone I know – how are they letting me down now?

I decide to drop the last couple of inches.

I let go and fall eight feet to the ground, hard.

I land on the balls of my feet then fall backwards onto my bum and elbows: classic gymnast's dismount. So *where* was the water butt? I stand up quickly and bash my shoulder against it. Oh, there it is, a quarter of a millimetre to the left. Great work, Lou. That's going to bruise.

I'm really late now, but as I step forward I crash into something big and confusing. It's metal, with loads of sticky-out bits that hit me in the stomach, legs and face. I lose my balance and fall on top of it.

I fight it for a while; it seems to be covered in moving parts. Is Dad building a *torture machine* out in the middle of the garden?

I can't believe it – he's usually so fussy about tidying things away. And he's not a psychopath.

I finally fight off the Machine of Pain, adding a few more bruises to the collection. It's been a pretty unstealthy few minutes, and I can picture Lav standing at the bedroom window, shaking her head and wincing at every crash as her idiot sister pratfalls over everything she can find.

I stand and wait for my eyes to adjust to the darkness. It was an upside-down bike. Of course it was. Something else that Dad's "repairing". Once I can see better I feel my way out of the side gate and start running.

I'm a fast runner, and without a bag full of books I make great time sprinting along the road. As I approach the pool I can just about make out the three boys loitering in the gloom, impatiently pacing around the car park. Pete's fiddling with a cigarette packet but not smoking.

I bound up to them and they all jump about six feet in the air.

"What are you doing?!" Roman snaps.

"Ah, did I fwighten you?" I snigger before shyness can stop me. Surprisingly, Pete laughs.

"I'm sorry!" I tell them all. "I couldn't get away sooner! I had to wait for my mum to leave and then fake a … an illness for my dad."

"Why?" asks Roman, baffled.

I stare at him. "Because I'm fifteen."

Gabe laughs. "She can't just stroll out the house, like: *Don't wait up, guys, I'm taking the car!*"

"You're fifteen?" says Roman incredulously.

"Yeah."

"You look *much* older," he says, in a way that doesn't feel like a compliment. But fine.

"Right," Pete says, bored of this chit-chat and snapping on a professional-looking torch. "Follow me."

We walk past the swimming pool and through one of the school fields, which is just behind it. It's seriously creepy. I wouldn't do this alone, but Roman and Pete lead, with me and Gabe following. Roman doesn't seem to be able to let the age thing go.

"Did you know she was only fifteen?" he asks Gabriel.

"Yes," says Gabe, "she's in the year below me. The year that fifteen-year-olds are in. I didn't think she was a twenty-year-old who couldn't pass her GCSEs."

I snicker. Gabe's so funny, he might even be funnier

than Hannah. Oh, *Hannah*! I haven't had a second to email her again with something better than "Everything will be OK, here's a stuffed owl with its head on the wrong way." I will do it when I get home, even if I'm dropping with tiredness and it's 5 a.m.

We reach the edge of the field and Pete leads us into a dark little wood. He marches through it and we all follow like obedient ducklings.

It comes out into what looks like an industrial estate, and Pete heads down an alleyway towards a large concealed doorway.

Pete fiddles with the lock and carefully pushes open a heavy metal door. We follow him in. We're in pitch darkness, but the air feels warm and there's a weird smell. Also a humming noise. *Where* is this? I follow Pete closely. It's *so* dark in here. I reach out and pinch his jumper gently. I expect him to tell me to get off but he doesn't, and Gabe hangs onto me in the same way.

There's carpet underfoot that's so rough my trainers are catching on it and making me trip. We take a few steps, then Pete suddenly turns right and I stumble over the back of his foot. I fall forward, putting my hands out to catch myself, but there's nothing there and I'm falling and falling into darkness and I don't land on the floor, I land on a sloping pane of thick glass. My hands slap down on it first, smooth and cold, followed by my head. Hard.

As my forehead smacks against the glass, the most nightmarish thing I've ever seen looms at me: cold, pale skin, stone eyes and rows and rows of teeth.

A shark.

It emerges out of the darkness and I think I'm going to die. I scream and scream and my head is throbbing. There's whooshing in my ears and I slide down the glass until I'm crouching, wrapping my arms around my head to save myself from those teeth.

And then I faint.

25

I open my eyes. I'm lying on the floor; the carpet is so rough it's like lying on Velcro. It's snagging my trousers and I notice in a dreamy way that it's giving me a wedgie.

My back is aching and I feel sick to my stomach, but there's something soft under my head and cool hands are cupping my face.

"Lou? Lou?" I feel breath on my cheek; it's Gabe's voice. He turns to the others and says in a harder tone, "Call an ambulance."

"We can't!" That's Pete sounding panicked.

"His dad will lose his job!" Roman is somewhere far above me.

"I don't care! Call an ambulance!" I've never heard Gabriel sound so angry.

"I'm here. I'm..." I'm *trying* to say, "I'm not dead, and *please why shark?*"

"Oh God, Lou!" breathes Gabe, sounding like his old self again. I feel a weight on my shoulder: his head. I put my hand on his hair. I feel like I should be comforting *him*, not the other way around.

"Are you in pain?" he asks.

"No," I lie. To be honest, between the water butt, the upturned bike and now this I am eighty-seven per cent pain. But, whatever.

"The shark!" I pull myself into a sitting position. My stomach churns. "Was ... did...?"

"We're in the aquarium," explains Gabriel with a shaky laugh.

The aquarium. Of course.

"You could've said!" I say in the general direction of Pete's voice.

"I wanted it to be a surprise," he defends himself, sounding uncharacteristically nervous.

"I was surprised," I say heavily from the floor.

I hear Roman give a tiny laugh and get to my feet slowly with Gabe's help.

"So now what?" I ask a little throatily. Standing up makes me feel like sick times sick, so I lean against a wall.

"Now," says Pete, his voice disappearing into the darkness, "this!" He turns on the lights in the fish tanks and the water glows with a bluish light. Small shoals of shining fish drift past the glass. It's the most beautiful thing I have ever seen.

We stand in silence and I find myself reaching for Gabriel's hand. To my surprise, Roman reaches for mine. It feels nice, like a family. I wonder if Roman and Pete are holding hands too. Best not ask. We stare in silence until Pete breaks the moment.

"Now, what would you like to swim with?" he asks, peering in to read the labels. "Koi carp, tuna or—"

"Swim *with* the fish?" interrupts Roman. "I thought you said there was an empty tank!"

"Yeah – there was, but now there isn't." Pete brushes it off as if it's not important.

"Sorry, Peter, hate to be dull," chips in Gabe, "but could we have a few more details on this?"

Pete sighs as if Gabriel is being ridiculously fussy.

"There was an empty tank, but it is E-M-P-T-Y. No water in it. So just for tonight we've got to swim with a few fish. It's fine, they're totally harmless. Shall we try tuna? I had a tuna sandwich for lunch, I feel like it's one nil to me already."

Well, someone's in a good mood, I think groggily. That may be the first joke I've ever heard him make. But ... hang on.

"Pete," I say, "tuna are huge and bitey."

"No they're not," he corrects me. We turn towards the tank and about twenty tuna fish slide past. They're the most thuggish-looking fish I've ever seen in my life.

"Yeah. They are," say Roman and Gabe in unison.

"Oh for f..." Pete sighs and runs lightly up a flight of stairs I hadn't seen in the gloom.

There's some activity above us, and the top of the tank slides to one side. We watch as one pale foot and leg appear in the water, then another. There's a moment of calm, then suddenly *all* the fish race towards them. It's so quick I yelp with shock.

In a flash, Pete yanks his legs out of the water, but those fish moved so fast, I don't know if he got bitten. They look furious, thrashing around at the surface of the water. I can't be sure but I *think* one of them is chewing.

"Pete?" Gabe calls quietly upstairs. "You all right?"

No answer.

"You probably ate a close friend for lunch, Pete, and they wanted revenge," I call up.

We wait a moment, sniggering quietly.

"OK, fine." Pete appears again at the top of the stairs, acting as if that incident never happened. He bounds downstairs. "Let's try another tank."

"After you, mate," Roman says, smirking.

Several nibbles and a couple of harrowing near-misses later (seriously, if you've got an octopus in a tank, LABEL IT, there's no point being modest), we finally find a tank near the back that's full of tiny brightly coloured fish who seem more scared of us than we are of them. We agree that we can only practise the underwater stuff – none of the lifts above water – but these things all need work, and the boys sink to the bottom of the tank and begin.

It is arresting to watch, and that's not just my concussion talking. The boys float in perfect unison in the glowing blue water, with fish drifting past them in bright flashes of colour. It's the most calm and eerie thing I've ever seen, and I feel a bit in love with all of them at that moment. Yes, even Pete.

I film their whole routine on my phone and I get the perfect take. At one point an eel swims in front of them! Thankfully, the boys are too absorbed in their swimming to spot it, or they would've freaked out. I watch the video back as they're getting changed upstairs and I'm completely absorbed.

I've got wifi so I upload the video to YouTube, and after a moment's thought I send Hannah the link. Maybe it'll be good for her to see there's life outside camp, that there are cool things happening elsewhere. I don't tag the boys or add any hashtags: let's keep it secret til try-outs. Nothing but bad has come of Debs discovering our secret. I don't want any more obstacles.

I notice a new email from Han. I can only see the preview, it says: I can't do this any more.

Hmm, is that in a dramatic "I'm running away" way, or more of a "Time for a new attitude, I must stop being so hard on myself"?

I keep refreshing my email to try and make it open. I feel quite anxious now.

I'm engrossed in my phone and oblivious to everything around me when suddenly Roman grabs me by the arm and shoves me and we're running, stumbling on the carpet and feeling our way along all the cold glass tanks. I'm stubbing my toes and fingers, banging my head and I don't know what's going on except I know I'm scared.

"Police!" Roman hisses at me and I feel cold with fear. *I'm running away from the police?* What has happened to my life?

The boys are running faster than I can keep up, even

Gabe. I'm still woozy from banging my head and I fall a couple of times and scrape my legs, but Roman won't let me go. He drags me up each time and keeps pulling me. I'm glad, because my head is thumping again and I feel so dizzy – there's no way I could do this by myself.

Now I hear what we're running from: heavy footsteps and dogs behind us. Pete suddenly darts left. There's the sound of a door opening and he lunges back and grabs my other arm, pulling me, Roman and Gabriel in behind him. It's a storeroom, I think. It smells of bleach and I see mops, buckets and a Henry hoover just before Pete shuts us in and we lose the faint aquarium light.

We are crammed tightly together. The boys are pressed against me on all sides and I can smell after-shave, sugary hair product and a little sweat. We're shaking with the effort of trying to breathe quietly. My head is against Roman's chest; I can hear his heartbeat. This is the closest I have ever been to a boy.

It's gone quiet outside and I hold my breath (as if that will help at all). I close my eyes, but this makes me dizzy and I take a small half-step back. I lose my balance, Ro grips my shoulder, and I'm grabbing at Gabe and Pete so as not to fall in a loud clatter of mops and buckets.

All four of us are sliding downwards, slowly and

gently. It would be funny if we weren't so scared.

We can't get caught. We'll be in so much trouble. I'll be grounded: no more training, no more friends. Pete's dad could lose his job... Please, whoever you are, keep walking.

I can't hear anything. Just the sound of us breathing. I feel really sick and the room is starting to spin.

Suddenly there's a bang as the door is flung open and we all recoil from blinding torchlight. The pressure in my head gets worse; I can feel my pulse thumping in my neck and I'm sliding further till I'm practically on the floor. Roman, Pete and Gabe all look oddly far away. Pete's lips move but I can't hear what he's saying. There's a rushing noise in my ears and blackness creeps in at the edges of my eyes to meet in the middle.

26

I wake up suddenly with a strange pressure over my chest. I can't move my arms. There's a rustling noise when I try. I realize it's because I've been the victim of a brutally hard tucking-in.

Why am I in hospital?

I turn my head and see Mum. She's rummaging through her bag and looks like she's been crying. Lav is standing behind her, unrecognizably serious, with faint mascara streaks down her cheeks. She catches my eye and her eyes widen. *What is going on?*

Mum's head jerks up and she gasps at the sight of me.

"Oh, Lou!" She bends down to the bed and hugs me tightly. "What were you doing?"

She breathes into my hair. She's gripping me hard, angry with relief. I've not seen this in years, not since that time I was seven and decided to have a snooze in the garage for a few hours without telling anyone.

Mum doesn't let go, and I'm breathing in her shampoo smells. I'm remembering the aquarium bit by bit.

"Where's my phone?" I ask stupidly.

"You're not getting that back in a hurry," comes a grim voice from the other side of the room. I've never heard Dad sound so strict. I turn my head to look at him. My neck feels stiff and tender.

"I'm sorry I sneaked out." I can't keep turning my head, so I address Dad and squeeze Mum's hand. "It wasn't Lavender's fault; I just needed to help the boys with their swimming training."

"Was that it?" Mum asks.

"Yes, of course!"

"Of course nothing!" Mum's temper flares up. "You were found in a broom cupboard with two older boys and a man who left school last year, unconscious and covered in bruises! We had no idea what had happened!"

I touch my face. It feels puffy and hard. Even lifting my hand sends shooting pains down my side.

"Do you want a mirror?" Lav asks.

Dad clears his throat. Lav and Mum look over at him. He obviously doesn't think this is a good idea.

Lav makes the decision and hands me a little compact mirror from her handbag. I put it up to my face and then angle it down my neck and shoulders. The cuts and bruises don't stop. My face is black and blue, I have a split lip and there are strange marks all over me. It looks like I've been fighting wild animals.

That makes me remember the shark, and I shiver.

"Are you OK?" Mum is watching me warily.

"Mum, this is all my fault."

"None of this is your—"

"No, I mean it *really* is – I snuck out, I fell off the water butt," I say, pointing at my shoulder. "Then I tripped over a bike in the back garden, then at the aquarium I fell over and I headbutted one of the tanks. I know I look like a horror film, but no one *hurt* me. This is all incredible clumsiness."

Lav is watching me, her mouth twitching as she fights a grin.

Mum still looks grim.

"Blame an upside-down bike if you want to blame something."

Mum shoots a look at Dad, who protests. "How did this become *my* fault?"

"Are the boys in trouble?" I ask.

217

"Yes," the three of them reply in unison.

"Can I have my phone?"

"No."

"But..."

"NO."

"I need to speak to Roman, Gabe and Pete! I'm coaching them for *Britain's Hidden Talent*, the try-outs are days away..." I trail off because Dad is shaking his head, eyes closed.

"No, Lou, there'll be no *Britain's Hidden ... Thing*. The boys will be lucky if they're not expelled, or worse."

Cold and hot runs through me. I feel weak, like the last bit of hope just leaked away. This isn't going to be all right, is it? Everything's ruined.

27

Lou, hun, are you OK? We heard you got ARRESTED with Ro Garwood and Pete Denners. That can't be true?!! Want to meet up after swimming training this week? All the girls were saying that we should, we haven't seen you in AAAGES!

Nic xx

Hi Lou, I just wanted to get in touch to see if you're OK. Call me if you'd like to talk, I can't imagine how you're feeling but I can listen.

Cammie says hi.

Melia x

Girls, this is Lou's mum. I have her phone until further notice.

The hospital discharges me first thing next morning and a young policewoman comes to our house later to drink coffee and point a sceptical face at me. Annoying. Mum gets out the crockery we only use at Christmas. It's strange to see it on duty in October.

No one will listen to me, and I'm starting to get really scared on the boys' behalf. I show the policewoman the water butt and the upturned bike, like the most rubbish guided tour ever.

I'm still not allowed my phone back. I totally forget about Hannah's unread email because I've got so many different problems: worrying if the boys got expelled; or, worse, if the police are involved. Any time I try to google the local news on our home computer, Mum is on me like a tuna fish on Pete's leg. Plus I've got these painkillers to help me sleep and they leave me groggy till the afternoon, so my days drift by in a frustrating blur.

I have to stay home from school for a couple of weeks to get over the concussion and "let things blow over", as Mum says. Saturday is the last public try-out. The day passes and, despite my begging, there's no way I'm allowed to go.

Mum and Dad won't even let me leave the house. They only manage to stop me by telling me if I go and see the boys they'll be in *even more* trouble and then that really will be my fault. So I head back to bed and cry until I fall asleep and I wake up with a face like a blister.

I wonder if the boys go to the try-outs without me. I bet they do. I have the most unreasonable parents in the world. Lavender reports back from school. She tells me:

(1) People are shamelessly nosy and she's told them all to eff off, especially Cammie, who reckons she's "distrawn" (not even a word).
(2) Roman is back in school but she hasn't seen Gabe.
(3) She's finally getting used to Amelia Bond's lack of hairy face mole, but it'll be a long road.

I suppose I'd rather Roman, Gabe and Pete went to the try-outs without me than miss out. But when I think about them getting into the final while I'm stuck at home I feel left behind. I have serious FOMO.

I wonder how Gabe could've done this for a year. I start going nuts after three days. Mum eventually lets me out for a drive with Dad after I start chalking up my days of incarceration on the bedroom wall with Lav's eyeliner.

Victory! (Though I have to buy Lav a new eyeliner.)

And, with perfect timing, my aching back and nausea turn out to be not aquarium-related, but in fact my first period. Mum brings me a hot water bottle.

"It's been a memorable week," I tell her.

"It's still not as traumatic as my first period."

"*Pffft*. How many police were involved in *your* first period?"

"None, but I was dancing in the school play. In white trousers."

She tucks me in with that horrible thought. I don't dare sleep in case I dream.

The next day I'm catching up on some homework that Mr Peters dropped round. ("Lovely guy, dark eyes," Mum said. "Bit skinny," Dad sniffed.) With a stomach jolt I remember Hannah's email. I cannot believe I haven't thought about her since the broom cupboard, but concussion is a funny thing, the doctor said. "Hilarious," I said, feeling my lumpy head.

I beg Mum for my phone. She's about to say no, but I tell her about Hannah's latest messages, about her getting more and more stressed and her parents putting loads of pressure on her. Dad comes downstairs and loiters behind me, making a sandwich and earwigging.

"I am going to look through your phone," Mum says, in a voice that expects me to argue.

"'K."

"Lavender would go nuts if you tried that with her," Dad mutters, head in the fridge.

I roll my eyes. "That's cos she has loads of boys begging her to go out with them and all *I* have is an argumentative synchronized swimming team."

Mum leans against the counter and scrolls through my phone. I look at her face for reactions.

"Anything?"

"Your friends from the swimming team want to know if you're OK, *babes*," she says wryly. "You've got two new emails from Hannah."

"Can I read them?" I say, getting up to look.

"No. Not after the week you've had." She begins to read.

Dad stands behind Mum and looks over her shoulder. Their faces become grim.

"What?" I demand. "Come on, she's my best friend!"

They read on. At one point, without taking his eyes off the screen, Dad reaches out and holds my hand.

I think he forgets to let go. It goes on a while as he and Mum are bent over my phone, heads almost touching as they scroll through all the older emails and still we keep holding hands. Am I going to have to drag him off to university with me?

"Hi guys, this is my dad, could you get the door? No, it's cool, we go through sideways."

Finally they finish and they look up at each other. Their noses are practically touching and for a mad moment I think, *Are they about to kiss?* They're not a couple, they had better not kiss. Plus Dad's still holding my hand!

Thankfully they don't kiss *and* he lets go of my hand. Double-win.

"What's a thigh gap?" Dad asks. I explain.

"Back fat?"

"Um..."

"Maybe fat that is on your back?" Mum says patiently.

"Right."

Mum catches my eye. I suppress a smile. She holds my hand and looks thoughtful. "So. It doesn't look like Hannah is coping very well with the pressure. Or that her parents are being very helpful." She pauses.

"What?"

They're clearly thinking something about me, I just can't tell what. Maybe the usual *I hope she's not going to get any taller.*

"OK," says Dad in his I Have a Plan voice, the one in which he usually announces his intention to experiment with pudding recipes.

He hands me my phone.

"Lou, you email Hannah and ask her what she wants to do. Tell her we can call her parents—"

"No," I interrupt him, "she will *flip out.*"

"Lou, she has already 'flipped out'. Read her thesis on back fat. So just be honest with her. And then..."

"Yes?"

"You can give me your phone back."

28

Dear Hannah, I'm so so sorry, I didn't realize you were going mental.

Hmm. Delete.

Hannah, I'm really sorry. I've been making new friends and I hadn't noticed you were

Even worse. Delete!

Hannah, I'm sorry, I didn't realize you were finding training camp so hard. It sounds like a really difficult place. Do you want me to tell your parents? Maybe you could talk to the coaches about slowing down your training? I'm sure if you told someone you weren't happy they would help you. It's easy to feel like winning is the only thing that matters, but I don't think it is. Take it from a loser! I'm sorry I've been so slow to get back to you – I've had a crazy couple of weeks. I'll tell you more later, please let me know you're OK!

Lots of love,

Weez xxxxx

It took me ages to phrase this, sitting at the kitchen table with tea cooling in front of me. But finally I think I've nailed it. I press *send*, then hand my phone to Dad, who puts it carefully in a box. He locks the box with a little key, which he gives to Mum, who pockets it with a smug face. Dad stands on tiptoes and pushes the box onto a high shelf in the kitchen cupboard that not even I can reach.

He turns back and stands shoulder to shoulder with Mum. They fold their arms – no one can take on Team Parent.

Almost immediately my phone makes a pinging sound and vibrates inside the box. Their faces drop.

"That's probably Hannah replying," I tell them, unnecessarily. Dad sighs and goes back to the cupboard and Mum digs in her pocket for the key.

It *is* Hannah.

DON'T SAY A WORD TO MY PARENTS. Seriously!
This means the world to them. But you're not a loser,
you know you're not. That video from the aquarium
was AMAZING, I've shown it to loads of people here!
I'm OK. I just feel low at night, things always seem
better in the morning. Gotta go... We're all off to the
cinema. Only joking, trainingtrainingtraining. LOL/cry.

Xxxxxxxxx

That wasn't the answer I was expecting. I don't like
how vague it is. Mum takes the phone, and she and Dad
read the message.

"OK," says Dad. "But I'd be much happier if we told
her parents."

"She'd be so angry at me. I already feel bad showing
this to *you*."

"Keep talking to her," says Mum, and hands me
back my phone. "I'm trusting you," she adds, hanging
on to it a second longer than she needs.

I head upstairs and spend the rest of the day googling
all the things I haven't known for the last week. It takes

ages. By the time I've finished checking "distrawn" (*knew* it wasn't a word) Lav is back from school and flopping wearily down on her bed, shaking her homework out of her bag.

"Good day at school?"

She sighs. "People are still bugging me about you."

"Can't they find out from Roman?"

"I heard this girl, Camo –"

"*Cammie –*"

"– is trying to flirt it out of him. He was quite rude to her."

I really enjoy that news for several reasons.

I sigh and catch sight of my stomach. I lift my top up and look at it. It's less muscly than it used to be. Cammie once said, "That would be so hot. On a guy." She's good at insulting me in a way that sounds like a compliment. Then I have to say thank you or else *I'm* rude.

I suck my tummy in and push it out as far as I can. Then suck it in again. Skinny. Fat. Skinny. Fat. Hate Cammie.

"What are you doing?" comes a wary voice from the other bed. I look over and Lav is staring at me over the top of a textbook. I pull my T-shirt down primly. Honestly, no privacy in this room.

"I have you on Eating Disorder Watch, just so you know," she informs me. "You've been on it since the time trials."

"That's sweet," I tell her. "I have you on Pregnancy Watch."

"Ha ha," she says good-humouredly. She puts down her textbook and rolls on to her stomach. Dammit, *everything* Lav does is elegant. Probably because she has much less body to control. I'm so lanky that when I move it's like trying to lead a school trip around the zoo – barely controlled chaos.

"I know you look different now you're not training, but it's OK, right?"

"OK."

"Don't you dare get an eating disorder. If you go bulimic you'll rot your teeth. If you go ano you'll get a hairy face."

"I *won't*!" I say, horrified.

"Uh-huh," she says authoritatively, disappearing back behind her textbook. "Your body goes fluffy everywhere, like granny's chin *all over*."

I think for a second, then hand over my phone with the thread of Hannah's latest emails.

"Does Hannah sound a bit weight-obsessed to you?"

She skim-reads it.

"Yes. Are you going to tell her parents?"

"I told Mum and Dad, but if we tell Barbra and Damian, what if they pull her out of the training camp? Then she won't get to be a swimmer and all her dreams will be ruined and it'll be all my fault because I *told*—"

"Lou, breathe."

"Sorry. It's very stressful to think about it; it must be worse to live it."

"Stop picking your lips, you'll make them bleed. You've made them bleed. Hannah sounds pretty messed up."

"Yeah, but I bet everyone there is messed up!"

She chucks me a tissue.

"Thanks," I say, dabbing my split lip.

"Well." Lav shrugs. "I would tell them."

"I think Dad wants to. Mum and I say no."

We both lie back on our beds.

"So it's a tie," says Lav.

"Hannah makes it three to two we don't tell."

"Hmmm."

I tap out a quick goodnight message to Hannah. It's so good to have my phone back.

I watch it send and I see she's read it immediately.

Some dots appear: she's writing. They go. She's stopped. They pop up again: she's having another go. I watch the dots.

"Don't watch the dots," Lav says wisely. "It's a rule of dating."

I put my phone down. She'll reply tomorrow.

29

Drafts Folder

Hi Gabe, are you OK? I'm OK. I'm sorry, I don't
know what happened.

Gabe, can we talk?

Hi Gabriel, what's going on? Everything is so weird
here.

Hi Roman, I don't know if you want to talk to me but

Hey Pete

I haven't broken my word to Mum, I haven't *sent* any

messages to the boys. I would, if only I could think of the right thing to say. Anyway, I'll be seeing them soon.

Yesterday, Mum and Dad said I can go back to school if I think it'll be OK. No, Mother, Father, bless your optimism, it will be *far* from OK. Lav says all anyone knows is that the three boys got arrested and I was there, and that could mean *anything*, right?

Bottom line: Loner Loser Lou Brown got three popular boys arrested. I can't see this raising my social standing much higher, but how much lower can it possibly go? I bet people will want gossip for a few days then forget about it, so I'll just keep my head down. Funny, after I've spent half a term desperate for anyone to talk to me.

I pack my rucksack the night before, and I feel something bulky at the bottom. It's *Swimming for Women and the Infirm*. The spine is flaking away: it's sat forgotten at the bottom of my bag since our last training session. The musty old smell of it reminds me of late nights at the swimming pool and I feel sad that all that is over. Even my shoebox full of twenty-pound notes makes me feel nostalgic. I'm not sure I'll ever have the heart to spend it. Lav offers to take it off my hands if it's too emotional. So kind, I tell her. But no.

I wake up early the next morning, and I'm eating

cereal as Mum and Lav come downstairs. They give me supportive looks but I just stare into my bowl – I'm not in a good mood. I sneak out *once* in fifteen boring, nerdy years and all hell breaks loose. Because when I rebel, I really go in with both feet.

Dad gives us a lift. He pulls up in the school car park and Lav turns back from the front seat.

"Want to walk in together?"

"If that's OK."

"Course."

She waits for me as I disentangle myself from the car and my rucksack. I'm nervous and clumsy and I can feel people's eyes on me. (Looking, not actual eyeballs. That would be gross.)

I finally step out of the car, my legs feeling a little rubbery as Lavender and I walk towards the front doors. People are definitely staring, and I'm blushing already. But Lav doesn't peel away from me to join her friends. She walks me right to my form room, and luckily we bump into Mr Peters in the doorway.

I feel like Lav hands me over to him as if I'm a package, but it's probably for the best. As I enter the form room some people stop talking and stare at me, while others talk more urgently, possibly *about* me. I don't look good: my face is still a mess of bruises and I have carpet burns on my hands and a nasty scab on my lip. I sit at an empty desk at the front rather than risk walking all the way to the back. I'm next to Mr Peters, so no one dares to approach me.

The people at this school are the worst – it's either ignore you or stare at you. *Find a middle-ground, weirdos!*

The bell goes for first lesson.

"Oi, is that a *bruise*?" some guy yells at my back as I race out of the form room, and I can hear a couple of girls gasp, scandalized but amused.

Three more years, Lou, I tell myself, hitching up my rucksack and walking head down towards my history class. Three more years, get your GCSEs, get your A-levels, change your name to Trixie McCool, go to university and deny that Louise Brown ever existed, let alone went to an aquarium after-hours.

I'm exhausted already. A week and a half in bed and I feel weak as a kitten. I snooze gently at the front of history with my Interested Face on. The teacher isn't convinced but she leaves me alone today. At my height I'm not one of life's natural sneakers, but today I do my best. I skulk in the toilet at break, then sit at the front for my next two lessons.

At lunch I'm heading to the canteen looking around for Roman and Gabe, but I don't see them anywhere. Instead I bump into Melia. She smiles, looks genuinely pleased to see me.

"Hey, you OK?" she asks, jumping straight in without any chit-chat. Seems odd, but then Cammie and the rest of them appear behind her, putting an end to any conversation.

"Oh my god *look* at *you*!" drawls Cammie. "Who did that? Not Roman? Did he *hit* you? Were you in an *accident*?"

People are turning to look, exactly as she intended.

Melia looks mortified. "Cammie," she murmurs.

"What?"

"Just ... forget it."

Well done, Melia, way to assert yourself. I take advantage of Cammie being distracted to nip past them.

I head to my old refuge, the library. I'm going to find the biggest book I can and hide behind it. If it's big enough I'll build a fort and refuse to come out till hometime. Immature, but that's my plan.

I turn into an emptier corridor and feel myself calming a little. Honestly, all this drama! The worst thing

I did was lie to my parents and maybe scare a few fish. There wasn't half this much fuss when Lav sneaked out to a party, trod on a nail and ended up in hospital in sequinned hotpants getting a tetanus shot. The injustice rankles.

Head down, I march quickly down the corridor. I turn a corner and walk straight into Roman – actually banging my face on him.

"*Owb!*" I say pitifully, pinching my nose. It tastes metallic, as if I might get a nosebleed.

"Sor..." Roman begins, but he falls silent when he sees it's me.

A mean voice in my head wonders if he'll say hi. Bearing in mind that he didn't talk to me at school *before* I got him arrested and nearly expelled. But a less bratty voice reminds me how he held on to me when we were running through the aquarium and didn't let go even when I was slowing him down.

"You look awful," he says, shocked.

A couple of boys from my year turn into the corridor, see us and openly stop and stare.

Roman glares at them and they remember they were on their way to something very important, actually, and bustle past.

"I know I do. It's this new shampoo," I tell him.

Roman laughs. He never laughs at my jokes. Perhaps it's a pity laugh, but I'll take it: I feel sorry for myself. Every time I speak, my lips tug at the scab on my mouth. *Bleurgh.*

"How are you?" I venture.

"I've … been better," says Roman carefully. I feel like he's hiding something from me, and also… "Stop talking to my scab, please," I tell him.

"God, sorry." He smiles. He's so handsome when he smiles, but I'm not thinking about that right now – I'm preoccupied with something else.

"Where's Gabe?" I ask.

"Ill," Roman says, his friendliness cooling. "With the stress, he's got ill again."

I feel like I've been kicked in the stomach.

"I… I'm so sorry."

"It's not *your* fault!" He seems almost angry at the thought.

"I know it's not my fault!" I retort. "I'm sorry for *him*, I mean. I like him, he's my friend. I don't want him to feel like he's got flu all the time and be so tired that his limbs ache and stuff."

"Did he tell you that?"

"Yes. Now where do you live?" I ask, getting out my phone so I can type in the address. I'm going to go and see him, I decide. Right now. Roman watches me.

"You want to see him?"

"Of course!" I say. "If that's OK?"

"I was just about to get a lift off Pete, if you…?"

"Will Pete want to see me?"

"Oh, shut up," he says, grabbing me by the rucksack and giving me a little shove. "We'll drop you back by the end of lunch."

Our strides match as we walk out to the car park together. I'm nearly as tall as him. I can see people watching us and begin to feel nervous.

This is one of the stupidest things I've ever done, and I've been really adding to that list this past couple of weeks. I'm cutting school with two boys who were recently accused of beating me up. In a cupboard. In an aquarium.

Pete is waiting in the car park in his Mini, having a cigarette. I guess we aren't training any more, but I still feel a prickle of motherly irritation at him. He stares when he sees me, flicks it out of the window and gets out of the car. I give him an awkward wave and I'm shocked when he comes over and gives me a hug.

He squeezes pretty much every bruise I've got, but that's OK.

Roman opens the passenger door, flipping the seat forward for me.

(This is SO cool! Or it would be if it wasn't an emergency dash to the sickbed of someone I really care about.)

"Actually, do you want front or back, Lou?" (And if it weren't physically impossible to get three lanky teenagers in a Mini.)

"Um."

I feel like the only way we'll all fit in is if we liquidize ourselves and someone pours us through the sunroof. So I take the back seat and we play a slow, careful game of Twister as eighteen feet of human being is folded up inside the car.

We get the giggles halfway through and this helps nothing but it makes me feel a lot better. I don't remember the last time I laughed. I think it was pre-shark.

30

Lav

Are you OK? Millie says you cut school with Roman
and Pete? You are aware this is the Worst Idea
Ever?

Lou

Gabe's ill, I've gone to see him. I'll be back by the
end of lunch!

Lav

OK. Stay away from fish.

We get to Roman and Gabe's house – Ro lets himself
in and Pete follows behind, clearly at home here. I suddenly feel a bit shy.

It's bigger than our house, I notice as I walk in, but not as swanky as Hannah's.

"Gabe! Lou's here, are you decent?"

"Lou? Really?"

"Yes! Get dressed!" I call up the stairs. I hope his mum isn't in, that was dangerously close to flirty.

Gabe is dressed but sitting on his bed surrounded by loads of books and a laptop. I don't hug him because it feels weird: he's in bed. Instead I sit on the end of the bed and squeeze his leg.

"How are you?" we ask at the same time, and laugh.

"Better."

"Better."

(Golden rule, never too many words with boys, even nice ones.)

The four of us sit and chat for a bit. I have to ask them: "Did you go to the try-out? I mean it's cool if you had to go without me. Fine. Really."

They all look awkward. Roman speaks first.

"Me and Gabe were suspended. I thought we'd be expelled; the three of us were nearly charged with assault and then Gabe got ill and we barely noticed the day of the try-outs."

"I told my parents!" I protest, shocked. "I said the

bruises were me being clumsy when I sneaked out and that I fainted because I was ... coming down with something."

"What were you coming down with?" Gabe asks, and Roman and Pete look at me.

Of course, *now* I have their full attention. When I'm trying to teach them how to dive neatly, no one listens, but for this they're all ears.

"Girl Things," I tell Gabe. "I was coming down with a case of Girl Things."

"Are you going to get better?"

"No. It's terminal. I may have to buy a dress."

"Anyway!" Pete interrupts. Clearly he'd rather talk about getting arrested than my fascinating biology. Fair enough. "You were unconscious for hours."

"We were really worried," Ro says sweetly.

"Yeah, for you *and* us," Pete puts in. "It looked like we'd abducted you and beaten you up. In an aquarium. Like weird, violent thugs."

"Did you not tell them the truth?" I ask.

They look at me.

"Hey, officer," Ro begins. "We were practising underwater synchronized swimming ... no, it's not technically a Thing, we made it up."

"And we broke into an aquarium …" Gabe adds.

"With a girl I only just discovered was a bizarrely tall *child* …" Pete splutters.

"Hey!" I protest.

"… to prat around in a fish tank with some eels," Roman concludes.

"The police didn't believe you, then," I guess.

"It sounded so mad, they drug-tested us!" Gabe says indignantly.

I can't help laughing. It does sound like a surreal excuse for breaking into an aquarium. Then I remember something that hasn't crossed my mind since hospital.

"Hey! Want to see yourselves swimming in the tank?" I ask. "I filmed it."

"No way!" Excited, they crowd around my phone, but it's being stupid and slow. The video is taking up too much memory.

"Hang on, I'll delete it."

"I want to *see* it!" Pete whines.

"No, it's cool, I uploaded it to YouTube. I didn't tag any of us in it," I add, seeing the looks on their faces. "No one from school will find it. You're still cool, guys, don't worry."

I find the URL in my history, click it and leave it

loading slowly, propped up against the window, and promise them they can watch it soon.

"You need a better phone," Pete tuts.

"Not now I've lost my job," I tell him.

I catch sight of the time and realize I'm already running late for my afternoon lessons. I have to get back! Just as I'm grabbing my rucksack and Pete is getting his keys, there's a bang of the front door. Roman and Gabe look at each other and I can tell it's a parent.

I hold on to my rucksack straps and feel nervous.

Light footsteps run up the stairs and a small, elegant woman pops her head around the door. Her eyes go straight to me.

"Um, hello, I'm Louise, hi!" I blurt.

I feel so awkward – I wonder if she thinks of me as the person that got both her sons locked in a police cell. It was a bad night for me, but I bet it wasn't one for her family album either.

But as soon as Gabe and Ro's mum sees me, she steps across the room and hugs me gently. My bruises thank her for that.

"Are you OK?" she asks.

"I am, yes, thank you. I'm sorry everything…" I trail off, unsure how to finish that sentence.

"I'm sorry my boys were so irresponsible," she says. "I know they would never hurt you, *but* they were thoughtless and that caused you to get hurt."

Nicely put. I feel like she's untangled a knot in my head and I start feeling less guilty.

"I have to get back to school," I say. "I'm sorry!"

"Yes, of course." Pete holds up his car keys.

"Can I jump in and pick up some homework?" Gabe asks. "I really need to get out of the house."

"OK," says his mum, but she points a warning finger at Pete. "Drive. Carefully."

Gabe gets up stiffly and pulls a hoodie on. We all head downstairs, me first. I don't want him to feel shy about me seeing how weak he is. We head out to the car.

Gabe gets into the car first and I clamber into the back seat next to him, trying not to shove my bum in his face.

Roman looks at him anxiously. "Are you cold?"

"I'm fine," Gabe protests, but Roman chucks a blanket over his legs anyway. I tuck it in tightly so he can't move his legs, just to be annoying.

We're pulling out of the driveway – really slowly, in case Gabe and Roman's mum is watching – when she appears at the front door waving my phone, which I'd left on the windowsill.

"Thank you!" I shout as she posts my phone through the window. "Nice to meet you!"

"I'll feed you next time!" she promises.

I grab my phone as it falls and see that the video has uploaded.

"Ah look, here you are!" I say, and hand it forward. "This is you guys in the aquarium." Ro holds up the phone so that he and Pete can see it in the front and Gabe can see it in the back.

The video begins. And the boys in the front suddenly lean forward, blocking our view of the screen.

"Oi!" I protest.

"Down in front!" Gabe prods his brother in the back.

"Wait. But..." Pete looks at Roman, then at us. "We've got over a million views."

We all bang heads as we lurch forwards to see. One million, three hundred and twenty-two thousand views!

"How ... just *how*?" They all turn to me. It wasn't me, I have barely any social media, it must all be down to other people. I look on my phone. It was chosen as a Pick of the Week on a couple of websites; some people stumbled upon it and shared it; an actor tweeted about it; a DJ and a model liked it... Basically, my little video travelled round the world rubbing shoulders with the stars while I was moping in bed with a hot water bottle. Mental.

Roman starts whooping and banging his seat, the roof, Pete... We all join in until Pete's poor little Mini is rocking and making noises of complaint.

I look behind to see if their mum has heard us. I want to tell Mum and Dad and Lav but first I hug our fame to us – just for now it's our secret.

"Who cares about *BHT*, eh?" I say.

"Damn right," says Pete. "A million people have seen us already."

"Thanks to you, Lou," says Roman unexpectedly. "You're a genius, I don't know how you came up with those ideas. I'm sorry we never said it before."

"I had help. From you guys and..." Feeling mischievous, I pull *Swimming for Women and the Infirm* out of my rucksack and flip it open. I can see from their faces that they recognize some of the moves.

"*Never* tell anyone about this," Roman says firmly, and Pete agrees.

"Deal," I say cockily. "If you pay my library fine. It's massive."

Gabe is still looking at my phone.

"Don't look at the comments!" I warn him.

"Why not?" Pete asks.

"Life Lessons 101: don't read what people say about you on the internet!"

"Wimp," he scoffs and scrolls down.

The comments are amazing. There are a couple of mean ones, and some people accuse us of fish-abuse, but mainly they say that Roman is gorgeous, Gabe's cute and Pete's got massive feet. I'd never noticed that before and I sneak a peek, but he catches me looking.

"Size fifteen," he says a little huffily.

When we get tired of reading nice things about the boys and the routine (which takes a while), we all sit back in our seats and breathe a happy sigh. One. Million. Views.

"At least something good came out of the aquarium," I say.

"Worth getting arrested for," Pete agrees.

"And suspended," Roman joins in.

"Relapsing," Gabe adds.

"I'm still having nightmares about sharks," I lie. "So I win."

"School!" Gabe says, catching sight of the time, and Pete starts the car again and prepares to drive off. A second later he stops, frowning at his rear view mirror.

"Is your mum OK?" he asks. We all look behind us to see their mum chasing down the road after us. But this time she's waving the house phone.

"I don't know," says Roman, "hang on." He gets out of the car and jogs back to her. She gives him the phone and watches him take a call.

Pete goes to join them, leaving me and Gabriel sitting in the back of the car like a pair of muppets.

"The seat in front of me doesn't tip forward, but I think yours does," he says.

"That's all right," I yawn. I suddenly feel so tired. I guess it's been my first day out of bed in over a week and a lot has happened.

Gabriel rests his head on my shoulder and I rest my head on top of his. The silence goes on and on but it doesn't get awkward, it's the most relaxed I've ever felt with a boy. I close my eyes. Despite wondering what's happening outside, the heat of the car is making me drowsy.

Suddenly Pete and Roman are rocking the car, opening the front doors and shouting. It's the worst way I've ever been woken up, *including* the time Gran's cat puked on my forehead. Gabe and I yelp and clutch each other. I let go of him very quickly as Pete and Roman smirk at us over the backs of the front seats.

"That was *Britain's Hidden Talent* on the phone. They saw our video, they love it and they want us to come and try out! We've got one more chance! I told them we've got nothing to swim in," adds Roman before I can open my mouth, "and they say don't worry about it, they'll sort it."

I'm awake now, really awake, and I'm clutching Gabe's arm again.

"Wh-when?" I splutter.

"This weekend. We've got four days."

I look across at Gabriel. He's smiling but already shaking his head.

"I won't be well enough," he says. My stomach sinks and I try not to show how disappointed I am. Just for one second it was like the last terrible fortnight had never happened.

"Hey," I say weakly, "that's OK. It's just a dumb TV show for—"

"No." He interrupts me. "*You* swim for me. You have to, you know everything I do and you're a stronger swimmer anyway."

"But…" I stammer.

"No buts. And you chose the Lycra so it's your

own fault you have to wear it."

I'm dry-mouthed with shock. But there's a familiar feeling in my stomach. A tangy, bubbly feeling. It's competitiveness. *Hello, old friend.*

The boys pile back in the car and we play drum 'n' bass loudly, shouting along to it with happy whoops. There are no words to drum 'n' bass. FYI if you're an old person reading this, it's basically noise, so you just shout what feels right. It's a lot of fun. Especially when it starts raining hard and the thundering on the roof adds to the deranged feeling.

I breathe in deeply. This car smells of hair product and empty Wotsits packets. I reflect that I will never smell a Wotsit again without feeling nostalgic for this autumn with my friends.

And then I think that that was quite a weird thought and wonder how many brain cells you lose when you headbutt a shark tank.

31

Roman

Lou, I've just realized you can't wear Gabe's competition outfit, can you?

Lou

No, Ro, because I am a girl and…

Gabe

Awks.

Lou

That's cool, I've got loads of costumes. If you're
sure you can't do it, Gabe?

Gabe

Sozzles. You'll have to be the TV star.

Lou
I feel sick.

Pete
Think how we feel, we've got to lift you out of the water. You're like a Gabe and a half.

Roman
What a gent.

Lou
Swoon.

Gabe.
No. More. Fainting.

I get back to school half an hour late for my afternoon lessons, but it's English and I guess Mr Peters assumes I was skulking in the library trying to stay out of the way of gossip, because he taps his watch but doesn't mention it. Mum's right, he does have nice eyes, I think, grateful I'm not in any more trouble.

Teachers seem to be lenient on me all week, probably because my face still looks so battered. This is useful because I'm back to nodding off in classes, thanks to swimming training every evening. Thankfully we're managing to avoid Debs as I'm sure she'd book out the pool every evening if she knew we were still planning to compete.

Gabe persuades Pete to be a "honey trap", which I find very funny once I discover what it means. Basically, Pete has to do some tactical flirting with Cammie to find out what she and her team are up to: practising in some swanky private members' pool that Nicole's dad owns. Whoop de doo for them. It leaves the public one free for us, at least.

I hear from Gabe, who hears from Ro, that Pete might go on a date with Cammie – he thinks she's "really sweet". Ha. Sweet like a *snake*, I tell Gabe, and hope the message heads back the way it came.

I suggest we train first thing in the mornings, too, but wow, if I thought Pete was a grumpy git normally, that's nothing compared to how he is in the mornings. We all agree never to do that again. As Gabe says, bundled up in jumpers watching from the bench, the routine will look a little wonky if one of the swimmers has killed the other two.

Pete has started driving me home from practice. Dad

was sceptical at first, but Pete waits till I get to the front door and then waves before driving off. Dad seems to appreciate the etiquette.

We're just coming back from our last practice when my phone rings. It's Lav. She doesn't bother to say hi.

"Lou, have you heard from Hannah?"

"No," I say, and then think. "Actually, I haven't – since I asked if I should tell her parents." I start to feel hot with guilt. "It's just so much has happened…"

"Someone's called the house phone a couple of times but hangs up when we answer. Have you had any missed calls from her?"

"No," I say. *Just* as my phone starts beeping with messages. I take it away from my ear to look. Six missed calls from Hannah. Argh! Great timing. We get no reception poolside. "Hold on, let me try her."

I hang up on Lav and call Hannah, but it goes straight to voicemail. I try a few more times, but either her phone is off or she's poolside too (highly likely). I glance up; we've arrived at my house and the boys are all looking at me. I explain briefly.

I jump out of the car. To my surprise, the boys follow.

"Can we do anything?" asks Roman, helping Gabe out.

"I don't know," I say, honestly. "I don't know what's going on." I'm fumbling for my keys. Mum's already opening the front door. "Mum!" I say. "This is Roman and Pete and Gabriel."

"We met," she says icily. "At the police station."

Well, *there's* an introduction. I look back at the boys. Pete and Roman smile like they've been sick in their mouths but Gabe sways a little and puts his hand on the wall to steady himself. Mum steps forward.

"Come in," she says, and I think it's going to be all right.

Meanwhile, the Hannah situation is so far from all right that "all right" is just a tiny dot on the horizon. Apparently, she finally spoke when she last called the house. She told Mum that she wants to leave the training camp but doesn't want her parents to know.

"So she's going to run away?" I ask, baffled. "But surely the camp would call her parents as soon as they realized she was gone. And where would she go if she didn't go home?"

"She's not herself," Mum says. "She sounds completely overwhelmed and panicked. I'm worried she might do something stupid. I'm sorry, Lou, we need to tell her parents. Your dad's on the phone to them now."

Poor Han. As soon as my life improves, hers goes rubbish and I'm having too much fun to notice. Bad friend.

Mum makes everyone a cup of tea and forces Gabriel into a couple of jumpers. He says if we get bored we can play Pass the Parcel with him. Pete and Roman decline. Lav waggles an eyebrow at me.

Shut up, my flared nostrils say back to her. I do not want to unwrap him.

We're all squeezed into the tiny kitchen. I'm sitting on the worktop with Lav perched on the fridge, while the boys loiter in whatever space they can find. Dad is on the phone, pacing around the living room. I feel reassured with him in control; he's always been good with Hannah's mum. He says his tactic is to show no fear and try not to blink.

Mum picks her way through boy limbs to stand next to me. I rest my chin on her head and hug her. She feels small like this, but she still smells of Mum: moisturiser, dry shampoo and fabric conditioner.

"I'm glad you're not at the camp!" she says. I give a little shaky laugh. I feel the same.

"Glad I've got slow arms?" Debs would have a fit if she could hear us.

"Yes, Goldfish," Mum says into my hair.

We break apart. Gabe pretends to be sick into his jumper.

Dad has now paced out into the garden. He looks annoyed and is gesturing forcefully. He accidentally deadheads a few roses.

"I wonder if they're angry at us for not telling them sooner?" Mum wonders. "He'd better not punch my geraniums."

She remembers the boys suddenly.

"You know what you need?"

"I'm OK for jumpers, thank you," says Gabriel, a little muffled.

"Soup!" she declares and heads for the cupboard. "Now, if I mix tomato and vegetable, will it be nice?" she muses.

"No," everyone answers.

Only Mum could ruin tinned soup; this is why Dad does all the cooking.

A few minutes later we're all drinking soup out of mugs because there are too many people in here to open the cutlery drawer. When I finish taking another slow sip I can see Dad hanging up and stomping across the lawn towards us.

"Uh-oh," I say.

Dad comes through the doorway with a halo of cold air and the smell of garden clinging to him. He takes a deep breath and looks at the phone.

"Hannah's parents think she's being 'melodramatic'," he tells us. We all do surprised Big Eyes at him and then each other.

"What? Did you tell them about the emails?" I demand.

"We sent them over," Dad says. "They read them while I was on the phone but chalked it up to teenage angst and a bit of jealousy on *your* part. Apparently this is Hannah's chance of a lifetime and she has to stay there and tough it out. I said I think she's actually quite ill, and if she's not she will be soon, but they're not listening."

I thought Hannah's mum and dad would flip out and I'd be in trouble for not telling them earlier. I should have remembered they're weirdos.

"Then *we* have to go and get her," I say. It's a mad plan, but it's the month for that, and of course we have to – we're the only people who know her mum and dad are officially Awful. "Essex to Dorset isn't *that* far, surely?"

Everyone looks at me.

"Not that far," I persevere. "I mean, I'm not planning to walk it, I'll need a lift, but..."

Mum runs a finger over her eye. "I don't know what to do for the best," she says, sounding uncertain. Very unlike her.

"I'll drive to Dorset," Dad declares, "if Hannah's dad won't." This is very unlike him. Bold, bossy and a bit competitive. Mum looks gratefully at him. Everyone's gone mad this evening.

"We'll come," says Roman unexpectedly.

"Ah, now I don't think that's a good idea after your recent brush with the law, son," says Dad, not unkindly.

"What if you need some muscle?" says Pete, getting to his feet and looking suddenly very manly.

"That's why I'm taking Louise," says Dad.

Pete looks stubborn. "I don't want to be in the way, but I'd like to help. After the trouble we've already caused you."

Dad gives him a nod and Mum says firmly, "Not Gabe." Gabe doesn't object: he has dark circles under his eyes and is resting his chin on his hands. Mum will drive him home and explain to his parents where Roman has gone. She asks if she needs to call Pete's parents, and he laughs. I can't imagine Pete Senior is a stickler for bedtimes.

Roman, Pete, Dad, Lav and I all pile into Dad's car and head off down the motorway. My stomach is fizzing with excitement. I'm worried about Hannah, but I'm so glad we're finally actually dealing with it – and I can't wait to see my friend.

Plus, it is *so cool* heading off on a rescue mission late at night! There's Dad and Pete in the front; me, Lav and Roman in the back. Lav's in the middle as she's the smallest. She's sharing a blanket with Roman. They make a really beautiful couple. I catch her eye in the rear view mirror and she gives me a prim face that makes me smile into my scarf.

Plus, we're driving all the way to Dorset, and it's like three hours there and three hours back! This is proper holiday driving, and it feels a bit like a holiday: everyone's tired and eating sandwiches out of cling film.

I keep calling and calling Hannah, but her phone is still off. I remember her saying if it wasn't for me and Candy Crush she'd chuck her phone. I feel guilty, I haven't been in touch as much as I should lately. I text her.

Don't run, we are coming for you.

I realize too late that that sounds threatening.

PRISON BREEEAAAK!

After about an hour's driving we stop at a petrol station to grab fuel, crisps and biscuits. Within a couple of minutes all the snacks are gone and we're picking the crumbs out of our hair and laps. Roman and Lav are being very helpful to each other with this. *So* predictable. Well, they better not come running to me if feelings get hurt.

"Um," says Pete.

"Yes?" says Dad.

"Is Hannah a ... is she ... what size is she?"

God, is *everyone* looking to pull this evening?

"Lou, what would you say?" asks Dad tactfully.

"She's like me. Maybe bigger," I tell Pete.

"Outstanding," he says. "Because there isn't a seat for her. We've brought one too many people for a rescue attempt."

We all think about this.

"OK," Dad says finally. "If she's not nuts we leave her there. And if she's *really* nuts we strap her to the roof rack."

"Dad!" Lav slaps his little bald spot from behind.

"Oi!" he protests. "I'm a hero on a rescue mission. Show some respect and unwrap me a toffee."

32

We drive for a couple more hours, listening to a lot of songs that only Dad knows. There's a deep sigh of relief when we get near and he turns off the stereo "to concentrate". Finally his sat nav says we're there. It looks like a massive stately home. I had no idea the training camp was this plush; it looks like Hogwarts! A month ago this would've made me so jealous. I'm glad Hannah was too engrossed in her thigh gap to mention it.

The building is set back from the road down a driveway, with large iron entrance gates open in front of us. Dad hesitates then turns slowly in. We look around for a security guard in a hut or a sign saying RECEPTION or VISITORS THIS WAY, but there's nothing.

The car crunches up the dark gravel driveway.

"I feel like we shouldn't be here," I whisper.

"Well I'm not turning back now," says Dad.

"Shall we turn the lights off in case we wake everyone?"

"Good idea," says Lav.

Dad turns off his headlights and we keep inching forwards over the gravel.

"*Now* we look like burglars," Lav whispers in my ear. She has a point. I do hope the boys aren't about to be arrested for the second time in a month.

There's a sudden clunking noise and the car jolts to a halt. It's really spooky in the car with darkness all around.

Dad makes a puzzled sound and turns the lights back on. Everyone screams with fright at the woman standing in front of our car.

We've bumped into a statue. It's a stern-looking woman holding a jug on her head. (No wonder she's moody – she's using all the wrong muscles. Must be agony.)

Dad reverses slowly ... and she comes with us! Everyone makes a *Gah!* of shock. It looks like some bit of her is snagged on the front of the car. This rescue attempt is rapidly going wrong.

"Did anyone see that *Doctor Who* episode, 'Blink'?"

Lav asks and everyone shouts, "LAV!" crossly. Which I guess is a yes.

Pete tuts and gets out of the car to deal with Moody McJug. She's quite awkward to move and he obviously doesn't want to break the arms or the jug, so he hesitates for a moment then grabs a boob with each hand.

We all snort with laughter from the car. He gives us a look over her shoulder, like: *Oh, grow up.* But, no! Not gonna. Sozzlecopters.

Roman gets his phone out and leans forward to take a photo. Pete unhooks her from the front of the car with a scraping noise that makes Dad wince. He gets back in the car, bringing a waft of cold air with him.

"Did you get her number?" I ask. He gives me a sniffy silence while everyone sniggers. We carry on up the driveway. I try calling Hannah again, suddenly realizing that this rescue mission is going to be extremely difficult if our damsel in distress has calmed down and gone to bed.

It rings! She picks up.

"Lou!" she whispers. She sounds like she's got a cold.

"I was so worried, where *were* you?" I say. "Have you started running away or are you still there – I mean, here? Do you want to come home? You don't have to.

We can turn around and go back, but..."

Lav is making *slow down* gestures. There's a silence from the other end of the phone.

"Are you here?" Hannah says as if she can't believe it.

"Yes!"

"With my mum and dad?" she asks, but doesn't wait for an answer. "Yes! I want to come home."

"Can you see us on the driveway?" I'm whispering now too. I can hear her moving, pulling back a curtain.

"That's not my mum's car. Why have you come in a different car?"

Now is not the time to say, "Han. Bottom line: your mum and dad are a bit rubbish. Soz. Not all bad news, though, as mine are champions and we can share."

"Um. It's my dad's. Tell you in a minute. Can you come out? Are you going to tell them you're leaving?" I say.

"I'll leave a note."

"*It's not you, it's me?*" I suggest and she gives a little giggle.

Dad's mouthing something at me.

"Han, do you want Dad to come in and talk to your coach or something?"

"I can't face it. I will, but right now I just want to come home."

"OK. Meet you at the front door?" We hang up.

Lav and I get out of the car. Roman and Pete make to follow but Lav stops them.

"We'll go," she says. "She doesn't know you." The boys see the sense in that and sit back.

"Be quick, girls," hisses Dad. "This doesn't feel very legal."

"It's OK, Dad," I tell him, "I've watched a lot of TV crime shows."

We creep across the gravel, Lav holding tightly to my upper arm and guiding me towards the front door. I have terrible night vision, as a water butt and an upended bike can confirm. I still manage to trip over a couple of tiny statues.

"Stop that," Lav hisses in my ear. "Not again."

This tickles me and we're both snickering quietly as the large wooden door creaks open and then Hannah is standing there, silhouetted in the dim light from the hallway.

We stop laughing – she looks bad. (This is coming from me, who's covered in scabs and bruises.) She's thin and pale, with dark circles under her eyes to rival

Gabe's, and she's buckling under the weight of her bag.

I look to Lavender. I don't know what to say. I am fifteen. This is one of those times when I want to say, "Sorry, but I am a *child*. I'm going to bed to watch *The Simpsons* and dip some cookies in milk. If I can just leave you guys to tidy up this rather adult mess? Ta."

Lav doesn't let me down. Her year of seniority steps up and she reaches out a hand to Hannah.

"Han, this place looks lame. Shall we go home?"

Han gives a small noise, half-laugh, half-sob. Lavender takes her bag and I put my arm around her and we all head back to the car. I can see the boys pretending not to stare. I bet they thought this would be more action-adventure, less emosh.

As we walk, I can feel how skinny Hannah has become. Dad flashes the car lights at us and I wave back. He flashes again, more rapidly. Lav and I look at each other and wave at him again. Is he being cutesy? Time and a place, Dad?

He points behind us with Big Eyes, struggling to get his seatbelt off. We look over our shoulders and squint to see, running silently over the grass, two *massive* guard dogs.

All three of us jump and scream uselessly, then start

271

running towards the car, but we're running on gravel, which is slow. Lav is carrying a holdall and I'm basically carrying Han, who weighs less than the bag but is a more difficult shape, and there is NO WAY we're going to make it.

My legs feel like water. Are guard dogs trained to kill? Bite, anyway – definitely – right? Dad's car is now tearing towards us, spewing up gravel as he makes a sharp turn and cuts between us and the dogs.

Roman grabs me by the arm in a familiar grip and bundles Hannah and me into the back seat while Pete shoves Lav in the front and dives in behind her.

Thump.

Thump.

We all wince as we realize that was Dog vs Car.

Dad pulls the car around in a wide sweep and we race towards the gates. In the mirror we see the dogs giving chase again and two security guards bringing up the rear.

One of them takes something out of his back pocket and points it at the car. A red dot appears on the rear windscreen.

"He's got a gun!!" cries Lav, and everyone screams in terror and flattens across their seat. I feel Roman's protective arm over my neck, which is sweet but surprisingly painful as my knees dig into my eyeballs. When nothing happens I sit up slightly, pushing his arm away.

"Has he?" I ask. We all sit up, Dad keeping an eye on the gates but feeling around with one hand to check that everyone's all right.

"No!" says Han with a wobbly little laugh and we all relax.

"No," says Pete, "it's a remote gate thing." We look at where he's pointing and the massive iron gates, wide open a moment ago, are now closing.

"HANG ON!" yells Dad, flooring the accelerator. The wheels spin uselessly, flinging up gravel behind us and I feel a moment's concern for the guard dogs, who are having a really bad day at work. Then we suddenly roar forward at a stately 20 mph and burst through the gates, losing both wing mirrors in the process.

"Sorry!" Dad yells out of the window as the rest of us cheer and whoop and bang on the roof.

"Can we go back for my wing mirrors?" Dad asks.

"No," I tell him, "that was the coolest getaway ever! Let's not ruin it by creeping back, like: *Hi guys, did I leave my phone charger behind?*"

"Don't worry, Mr Brown," Pete pipes up. "My uncle's a mechanic, he'll sort you out."

We drive back through the night, slowly because it's dark and rainy and Dad has to lean forward over the wheel to stare intently at the road.

"Hannah, this is Roman and Pete. They're the synchr— swimming team I mentioned." (I still can't call them a synchronized swimming team without imagining them in flowery rubber swimming hats. It would make this prison break seem so much less cool.)

Lav calls Mum, Roman and Pete call their parents and I see Hannah take out her phone and look at it thoughtfully. It has fourteen missed calls from me and *one* from "Home".

"So… My parents didn't believe you?"

Dad peers even harder at the road. Roman and Pete become very interested in the interior compartments of the car. Pete even opens the glove box with an engrossed air, like: *A box for gloves, eh? This I must see…*

"Well, they thought maybe it wasn't as bad as it seemed," I say diplomatically.

"They need their bloody heads knocking together," says Dad, less so. "Don't worry, Hannah," he adds, "you can call them in the morning and stay with us as long as you need to. My wife is very accommodating to waifs and strays. Me, for one."

Lav reaches across Roman and pinches my leg.

Wife, eh? In-ter-esting...

On the way home we swing into a 24-hour drive-through. I get a big meal and shake my chips into the side of my burger box, then put it over Hannah's lap and mine equally. She doesn't eat a lot and she chews in a dry-mouthed way. That's OK, baby steps.

I want to talk to her about everything, but not in front of Roman and Pete. I've turned up with cool new friends and I don't want her to think I've told them all about her. She's still my best friend. I squeeze her hand.

I don't remember much more of that night; it's a blur of steamed-up windows, the rumble of tyres and the farty smell of old burger. I remember being helped out of the car and waking up just long enough to check that Hannah was all right. But my head was starting to throb and my aquarium bruises were niggling. It was a relief to crawl into bed.

33

I wake up in a strange position on the edge of my bed. I can tell I haven't had enough sleep, and there's a dampness to the air that screams, IT'S TOO EARLY, GO BACK TO SLEEP!

I turn my head slowly and … AARGH! I'm nose-to-nose with Hannah, her eyes shining in the dim light. I laugh silently and she smiles.

Sorry, she mouths.

I whisper slowly and carefully, "Are … you … less … mental?"

That does make her laugh. She catches herself before she makes a noise. "I feel much less mental," she says. "Those boys were cool."

"My boyfriend and my ex-boyfriend," I explain.

She grins.

"I am offended," I tell her, "that you didn't believe that for a *second*."

Lav croaks from the other side of the room, "If you don't shut up I'm taking you both back to the nut house."

"Sorry, Lav."

"Sozzles."

It's early but there's movement in the house and I can hear people talking in hushed voices and moving around in the kitchen.

"Shall we get some breakfast?" I ask Hannah, and then wince. Bit tactless.

"OK," she agrees. "Aren't your try-outs today?"

Yes, they *are*. Ah, *that's* why everyone's up so early! In fact, are the boys still here? I race downstairs to see what's happening and bounce into the kitchen.

Pete and Roman are leaning against the sink dressed in my father's clothes. It looks like they're heading to a My-Dad themed fancy dress party. Gabriel is sitting at the kitchen table, busy on his phone. He must've just come over. Mum is loading the dishwasher and Dad is loading up the car. How weird. Apparently I had a sleepover with Roman and Pete.

If you'd told me last term that this was in my future I'd have given you a glass of water and made you lie down.

Pete catches sight of me and stares, his jaw dropping. "Well –" I coiff my hair demurely – "they *are* nice pyjamas, thanks for noticing, Pete."

"WHY ARE YOU NOT DRESSED AND READY?" he bellows at me.

"What sort of a coach *are* you?" Ro joins in.

"One that's had four hours' sleep!" I yell back, but I'm already racing back up the stairs.

I'm glad Mum and Dad saw that; after all their worrying about me hanging out with older boys, they can see I've just ended up with three bossy employers.

I jump in the shower and spot Lav's face wash. Maybe I'll make a bit of effort today – we might get on TV! There's a sudden banging on the door. I freeze, mid-lather.

"Are you using my face products?" comes Lav's voice from the hallway. It's eerie. How does she know? What a useless psychic ability.

"No-oo," I lie. She's not fooled.

"Avoid your eyes and pay particular attention to your jawline. I've noticed that's where you get breakouts." Charming. But I do what she says, with careful, unfamiliar gestures.

Showered, I sprint out of the bathroom and into

my bedroom, yelling, "CLOSE YOUR EYES, CLOSE YOUR EYES!" as I whip off my towel, pull on my swimming costume and go to grab some clothes from my drawer. But the drawer is empty.

If Mum has washed the few items of clothing I own *together*, then I'm in my newest nightmare and going to BHT with nothing on.

Hannah is lying in bed watching me panic.

"All my stuff is dirty, but you're welcome to it." She points to her bag. Creased clothes spill out of the bag as if it's puking. That is my last resort.

I run my eyes all over our messy room vainly trying to find something I own before I have to beg Lav for help. She has been very nice lately, but I doubt she'll lend me something to wear. The last time she did, everything got covered in blood and mud and was cut off me in the hospital.

"Come on, Lou!" shouts Dad from downstairs. Well, someone's really getting into the spirit of things – only two weeks ago he was very lukewarm about my swim club.

"INNAMINUTE!" I yell.

"You're not as muscly as you used to be," Han says, watching me.

"Good thing, bad thing?" I ask, because if now is the time for a heart-to-heart about body image we have to do it *fast*.

"Good thing," she says, sitting up and pinning back her hair. "You actually look like a *girl*."

Eurgh! I make a joke disgusted face and she makes it back. When we were in swim club, the worst thing to happen to a swimmer's times were boobs and hips.

Which reminds me.

"I got my period," I tell her.

"Oooh." She looks intrigued. "Was it … OK?"

I pause, thinking about the aquarium, the hospital and the police. It's probably a story for another time. I'm sure most periods are less dramatic.

"Are you coming to *BHT*?" I ask. "We'll have to queue for about a hundred hours so I can tell you then."

"My life." She rolls her eyes. "I get to choose between queuing in the rain talking periods or seeing my parents."

"Good luck with your parents."

She makes a jokey grim face and tells me she'll come and meet us afterwards. Then she grabs a towel and heads for the bathroom, walking past Lav, who's standing in the doorway with a pile of clothes in her arms.

"OK," Lav begins, looking uncharacteristically

nervous, "don't yell at me, and I kept the receipts, but...
I-took-your-money-out-of-your-shoebox-and-bought-
you-new-clothes. Are you angry?"

"No way, I *hate* shopping! Gimme!"

"How can anyone hate shopping?" Lav wonders, as
if I'm a constant mystery to her.

I start searching through the clothes. "You haven't
got me anything in pink, or a *dress*?"

She's shaking her head scornfully. Sure, she's not an
idiot.

I put on a pale green shirt; it's crisp and smells like
a shop. Then I try and pull on some jeans. Oh, Lav.
Skinny jeans?

"You have to lie down and pull yourself into them,"
she explains. I give her a hard look, lie down and haul
myself into the jeans.

I bet there are bank vaults easier to get into.

"They'll look nice," she reassures me as I squirm on
the floor. "You've got a lovely body."

"You say that like I found it in a ditch," I grumble, but
finally I'm in my denim prison and racing for the door
when Lav slams it shut and positions herself in front of it.

"Two minutes," she commands, and I'm too surprised to argue. She comes at me with her hands up like

a cartoon bear and runs that oil stuff through my hair again. Then she holds me hard by the chin and a mascara wand is suddenly darting at my eyes.

"Laa-aav," I whine, "I've got to swim."

"It's waterproof," she sighs, and finally releases me to race down the stairs.

Mum, Dad and the boys are waiting impatiently in the hallway.

"Pete's so jittery he's already spilt two cups of tea," Dad says. "So I'm driving."

"And I'm coming too." Lav appears behind me. "For support," she twinkles innocently and darts a look at Ro. Hmmm.

Mum waves us off, probably desperate for some peace and quiet, and we all wedge ourselves back in Dad's car. He delegates separate responsibility to each of us to look behind, left and right as he doesn't have wing mirrors any more.

We drive to the conference centre with only a couple of near-misses, which happen when Dad is changing lanes and the human wing mirrors are checking Twitter.

The queue looks even bigger than last time. I dread to think how smelly the people are at the front of this one.

I feel the mood in the car sink a little, so I give a little chirp on my whistle.

"Come on, team," I say cheerily, "third time lucky." We carefully unfold ourselves from the car, Roman and Lav with some reluctance. Honestly, between Mum and Dad, Lav and Roman it is one big sex party round here.

We walk towards the entrance, wondering if we'll have to queue again.

"Nah. They invited us," says Roman in reasonable tones. "Who invites a guest round, then makes them queue at the front door?"

We dither a moment, then hear, "Hey! Guys?" from behind us – it's the security man from last time, the one who talked to his wrist. He was surly then, but now he's practically *beaming*. Is he drunk? Does he think we're someone else?

"Morning, morning, morning!" He bounces up to us.

"*Hiiiii*?" we reply doubtfully.

"We *love* the video here," Wrist Man tells us. "Such big fans."

"Thanks!" I beam back at him. Lav looks amused. Well, she's used to people sucking up to her. (I'm not, and it's *lovely*.)

"Have you seen all the remixes?" Wrist Man goes on. "I adore the track that Belgian DJ added to it. Is he a friend of yours?"

"I have no idea," I reply. *About anything you just said*, I want to add.

"Have you got representation?" he asks.

We look at each other, baffled.

"An agent? Or a manager?" he presses.

"Um, no, because what we do is, just sort of dance underwater in a community pool," says Gabe carefully.

"Should the kids go straight inside or speak to anyone first?" asks Dad, making us sound like we've just turned up for a ten-year-old's party. Showbiz!

Wrist Man leads us into the aircraft hangar. Immediately there's a camera in my face and a microphone even closer.

"Louise Brown, the Aquarium Boys' coach!" says a man I don't recognize. "We hear there was some police trouble after your video was shot; what was *that* all about?" he asks with a mischievous smile.

"Ah, well," I hesitate, sifting through all the insane details of that week and rejecting most of them as Too Harrowing for Chit-Chat.

Pete pulls me away by the arm and me, Dad, Lav and

the Aquarium Boys keep following Wrist Man. He leads us onto the stage. Lav and Dad hang back as we step in front of blinding bright lights. We all blink and bump into each other. Wrist Man gives us a thumbs-up then abandons us.

"Hello, guys!" comes a voice from the darkness out front.

"Hello...?" we shout back doubtfully, shielding our eyes to see a table with three chairs behind it and a woman with an earpiece and a clipboard waving exaggeratedly at us.

"OK, guys, real quick," she says, ticking off with her fingers as she goes through a list:

"You'll be prepped at the side of stage."

(What's prepping? *Will it hurt?*)

"You'll come on,

do your routine,

wait for the judges to give you their feedback,

then off.

Quick off.

It'll be *loud* in here with the audience, be prepared for that and DO NOT swear on camera."

"'Scuse me," I mumble. My mouth is dry and my tongue has gone big. "*Audienthe?*" I ask, but she's gone.

We all look at each other, then, "Clear the stage, please!" a voice booms from nowhere. Sorry, sorry, sorry.

We walk off and go to stand in the shadows with Dad and Lavender and have a small nervous breakdown.

"This is not another public try-out," Pete says.

We all shake our heads silently.

"What?" says Lav.

"This is the televised auditions," Ro says.

We nod. Lav and Dad's eyes go big.

"That queue," I say. They all look at me. "That queue. It didn't have any ferrets in hats in it…"

"Are you all right, Lou?" Dad asks, feeling my forehead.

"You're right…" Gabe says faintly.

That gigantic queue snaking halfway around town is not contestants, but the audience.

34

Lou! We heard you guys are off to BHT today, that's
beyond cool. Hook us up with some tickets?
Ten should be fine. I'm having a party this weekend,
sorry babes, forgot to invite you earlier, aargh, ditz!
See you at BHT!

Imogen (Lavender's friend) xxxx

I know who Imogen is, she's acknowledged my exist-
ence *once* in six years. Twice now. I read her text and
turn my phone off. I have more important things to
worry about. We now have to wait three hours, which is
really useful time in which to feel sick and pace around
a lot. Roman nearly twists his ankle tripping on camera
cables so we force him to sit down. He mustn't get hurt,
we're all out of substitutes now.

The term "dressing room" is too grand, but we definitely have a small room with no windows to ourselves. Plus there's a sign on the door saying THE AQUARIUM BOYS surrounded by stars. Gabe gets out a pen and changes it to: LOU BROWN AND THE AQUARIUM BOYS.

Lav calls Mum to tell her things have got "a bit out of hand", which is one way of putting it. Mum and Hannah race along to join us, and Wrist Man brings them up to our room to wait with us. Roman and Gabe's parents are at work, and I think Pete is a little embarrassed about telling his dad. He just says, "Let's see how the day goes."

The mood in this room is like a shaken-up can of Coke. I try to calm them down. Coach to the rescue.

"Come on, guys, do some stretches, stay limber!" The boys look at me, Gabe with a half-smile, and I remember – I'm swimming too.

It's like someone just added Mentos to this can of Coke.

I step outside to use the toilet, but really I just need a moment by myself to calm down. On the way back, I pass doors with signs on like ours. Pete is loitering in the corridor. I realize he's waiting for me. He nods his head at one of the doors.

The sign says PRETTY IN SYNC. I don't get it. He smirks and opens his mouth, then the door opens and Nicole appears in the doorway.

"Oh!" She's surprised to see Pete and I think I am literally invisible to her. "Pete Denners?" she says loudly, clearly meaning everyone in the room to hear. "Are you waiting for Cammie?"

"Nope," he says honestly. "Bye, then!" He grabs me by the arm and rushes me back to our dressing room.

"But I thought she was 'sweet'?" I tease.

"Sweet like a *snake*!" he says. And maybe it's bitchy, but I'm glad the message got back to him.

Someone knocks on the door and we shuffle aside to let them in. Our visitors turn out to be three very pretty – very orange – girls.

"Guys," one of them smiles, "we're here to give you a bit of make-up for the cameras." Her eyes roam over everyone in the room, resting hopefully on Lav.

"It's those three," says Gabe, pointing us out. The make-up artists hide their disappointment and set to work on our tired faces.

It's a strange feeling having little brushes dot and stroke my face. After about ten minutes my make-up artist steps back, satisfied, and I peek around her at the mirror. For the first time ever I look like I might be related to Lavender.

My new vanity deflates with a farty sound as I notice Roman and Pete are wearing more make-up than me and they look like supermodels. Sigh. This is the most beautiful I have *ever* looked, but still the boys are prettier.

Hannah catches my eye in the mirror. *You look amazing!* she mouths at me.

"You could look less surprised," I tell her sternly.

There's a sudden thundering of loud music from down the corridor.

"They're getting ready to begin," says my make-up artist, giving me a Be Brave look. I give her a Step Back Because I Might Be Sick On You one in return. She steps back.

My face feels stiff with waterproof make-up. "Ank oo," is all I manage as the three girls wish us luck and leave.

I can tell I look scared because Pete's being nice to me.

"We're going on in about an hour," he says gently, as if I'm a dog waiting at the vet's. "Do you want to watch the first part of the show from the side of the stage?"

We pad along the corridor, barefoot and wrapped in

towels, with Gabe, Hannah and my family in tow. I was sure I had mastered walking some years ago, but now my legs are all rubbery and they feel about eight feet long. We reach the backstage area and the guys with earpieces wave us through. They seem to know who we are, which makes me feel a little better, as right now I don't think I can remember my surname. I haven't felt this nervous since the time trials.

Unhelpful memory. Shush, shush, shush, Lou.

And, unlike at the time trials, this time I have Mum, Dad and Lav with me. The earpiece guys make way for us and point at a gap in the curtain where we can peek through and watch the show. We all step carefully, trying to not trip on all the stage equipment on the floor.

I bend down to put my face next to Pete's; he moves the curtain so I can see. (*Stop being nice, it's freaking me out!*) There is a lady onstage who looks like someone's mum dancing around with a ribbon on a stick. I can't see the audience, but I can hear them openly laughing at her. I reel back slightly: what is *wrong* with people?

I hang back and find I'm next to Dad, who puts his arm around my shoulder and whispers in my ear, "You don't have to do this."

"I kind of *do*, though, don't I?" I whisper back.

"Well, yes," he admits, "but if you want to do a runner I'll go get the car."

We nod at each other. Deal.

The judges give their verdict on the woman and her ribbon and they are brutal, saying the worst sort of YouTube comments but to her face. I have a sudden urge to wash.

Next up, a father and son dressed as cows play pop songs on cow bells. Gabriel whispers in my ear, "Suddenly dancing underwater feels normal." I smile at him, or I try to, but whatever they sprayed on my face has left it rock hard and I wince and hold my cheek while he stifles a laugh. I haven't been this close to him since we were in Pete's Mini and I wonder if he's thought about that since. I totally haven't. Nu-uh.

The act finishes and the father and son disappear off the other side of the stage. Now a huge tank is being lowered down in six pieces. The moment the first piece touches the floor an army of people surge forward with tools to fix it all together. I watch them drag a hose onto the stage and start filling up the tank while they walk around checking all the joins and edges.

Soon the tank is in place, filled, and the show music booms into life. I hear the indistinct sound of a voiceover man announcing the start of the show, then, from the way he holds the last word for a long time, I can tell he's announced the next act.

Hang on, what? Is it us *now*...? They said we'd be fifteen minutes, maybe I've lost track of time? Aargh!

I throw off my towel and stumble forward. I have a terrifying moment of being blinded from the stage lights and then someone pushes me firmly aside.

Debs is holding me back by the shoulder while her team sashay past, their faces lighting up with practised plastic smiles the second they hit the stage. Cammie, Nicole, Amanda and Melia – all in matching pink swimming costumes.

For the first time all day I feel a real desperate desire not to do this, to just go home, put two chairs back to back, drape my duvet over them and eat cheese on toast under there.

I don't even catch Debs' eye, I just walk away back to my team, where Roman and Pete are standing there with grins on their faces. What are *they* so happy about? They'd better not still be excited about how "hot" Debs' team is. They lean towards me and take an ear each.

"You know her team already got through the try-outs weeks ago?" they tell me in stereo.

I nod.

Roman whispers gleefully, "Well, we heard her kicking off, yelling at some poor guy backstage because now there are *two* swimming teams and only one can go through today."

He raises his eyebrows at me. Us! The thought that anyone might think me and my team could be equal with Debs'... I'm astonished.

Debs looks back at me and I can't stop myself, I give her my broadest smile. Which, thanks to the face spray, isn't very big, but she gets the idea and looks royally hacked off as she turns back to watch the stage.

We hear whooping and cheering from the audience.

"It sounds like they're doing well," says Pete nervously. Well, duh. He and Roman step forward to watch, but I grab them both by the elbows and shake my head.

"You swim no one's race but your own," I tell them firmly. They hesitate but I know I'm right, I give them a Listen to Coach look and they do.

Because I am so wise *and* a massive hypocrite, I risk a peek when they're not looking. Debs' team are doing proper synchronized swimming. It looks good, really pro, perfectly in unison. Maybe I'm biased, but *I* think it's a bit boring.

Our routine is more exciting: in some places it's *too* exciting. Possibly downright dangerous? Hm. Let's just hope the substitute doesn't ruin it all. I suddenly feel sick, and either my throat has got very small or the air here is too big.

Their routine comes to a triumphant end. I hear loud applause and then it quietens down, but I can't hear the judges' feedback, just the rumble of voices. I push my ear to the curtain to try and make out words, but I'm almost knocked off my feet by the team striding confidently backstage and waving over their shoulders at the audience.

Their jubilant mood doesn't last as Debs looms out of the darkness like a shark.

"*What* was that dive, Melia?"

Ugh, I think to myself, I do *not* miss that.

I look back and catch Hannah's eye; she's clearly thinking the same thing. Debs doesn't even notice her one-time star swimmer standing in the shadows because she's too busy bullying her team all the way back to their dressing room. Like she used to do to me, back when she cared.

"OK," breathes Pete, interrupting my happy thoughts. "Showtime."

We snap our goggles into place. Gabriel holds out his arm and we give him our towels. I realize I'm still wearing the whistle, and after a moment's hesitation I take it off and place it around his neck.

"Good luck, Goldfish," he says and kisses me on the cheek (but sort of near the mouth). I think that might technically count as my first kiss.

That is one impressively hot blush I have here. You could cook an egg on my head. Come on, Team, focus! (And yes, I've decided to start calling myself Team.)

The stagehands finish mopping up the water, the music starts again and I hear the booming tones of the voiceover.

"Bwuuuur bwurrr BWWUUUURRRRR!" he shouts.

That's us, we're BWWUUUURRRR!

Roman strides out first, I follow, then Pete behind me. I feel calm all of a sudden. There's no point being scared, it is just going to happen now.

All my swimming training asserts itself and I start regulating my breathing.

You'd think it would feel weird being nearly naked in front of so many people, but it doesn't. I ping my swimsuit straps for luck, once right, twice left.

We climb the stairs up to the tank and my knees

shake with every step. My body feels unresponsive, as if I've borrowed it off someone for an hour. How do you *work* this thing? Where are the gears?

The three of us line up along the edge of the pool. I look down, then up, panicked – it's just a pool like last time. The sides are filled in! Please tell me this isn't going to happen to us again...

But then several guys appear from the side of the stage and in one dramatic move pull away the plastic boards surrounding the pool. There's a *whoomph!* and lights shine through the water, dappling the faces of the judges and the audience with blue glimmerings. The lights move slowly, drifting past the tank – it's like they're recreating the aquarium video. Hope they don't add an eel.

For the first time I catch a glimpse of the judges. I recognize them from the TV: there's two men, two women and they're all staring fixedly at us with slight frowns on their faces. What's this? they're thinking.

THIS is Lou Brown and the Aquarium Boys.

35

The music swells and fills the auditorium. We've spent weeks swimming to music from Lav's crappy little speaker dock, but this is like a fireball hurling out from the stage. I can feel the bass vibrating in my ribs!

We raise our hands above our heads. There's a hushed silence as we wait for our cue. I can't begin to think about how many people are staring at us from the silent darkness behind the stage lights, so I fix my eyes on the water and visualize my dive.

Which is perfect. I feel the boys hit the water cleanly either side of me and we corkscrew to the bottom, where everything is silent and calm.

We somersault backwards in unison and I speed up as the others slow down. I watch the boys carefully out of the corner of my eyes, then I rise up and they dive beneath me, push off from the bottom, hold a foot and a calf each and raise me into the air. I break the surface of the water and almost fall because I'm deafened by the roaring sound in the studio. Everyone is cheering!

The boys throw me up into the air and I somersault, knees tucked hard to my chest. I catch a quick glimpse of the judges' table before I dive down to the bottom and I'm back into the routine.

We swim around each other in a circle then Pete peels off to lie on the floor of the pool followed by me, then Roman. It sounds unspectacular but it takes such control. You have to let all of the air out of your body and we each exhale at a precise moment so that bubbles rush up from Pete, then me, then Roman. We slap our feet and upper arms on the bottom of the pool, push up hard and kick with mermaid legs to reach the surface. By now we have no air left in our lungs and it takes a super-human effort.

I always thought this would be the bit that drowned Gabe. I'd watch him do this with my heart in my throat, poised to grab him and pull him out of the pool, but he always struggled through. It makes my head spin and my ears ring – that's why we put it at the end.

We lie on our backs on the surface of the pool like

starfish with our arms and legs interlocking. We need this bit to get our breath back for the final push, so as the music builds we're panting and waiting for our cue. This is the moment where the bass swells, we thrust our arms above our heads and we dive backwards underwater.

The routine ends with the three of us motionless.

Arms crossed over our chests.

Underwater.

Heads down.

Boom.

It gave *me* shivers watching the boys do that, through misted-up goggles in our school swimming pool with verruca plasters drifting past – it must look incredible now.

We surface and splash towards each other for a painfully hard group hug, which is a lot of slippery naked skin on skin.

We break apart *prit-ty* quick.

Gabe falls up the metal stairs to hug Roman, who pulls him into the water and we're all hugging each other again. And then sinking, because that's how water works, and hugging and sinking again because we're too excited to think straight. I can't believe we've actually done it! I don't even care what the judges thought!

Well ... I do a bit. So we swim to the edge of the pool, panting and pulling off our goggles. The judges are laughing and applauding and the comedian is even wiping at his eyes.

"Well," says the mean one, spreading his hands wide as if he has no words, which makes the audience burst into roars and cheers again. It's deafening, actually painful to hear, but we're wincing and laughing.

"What even *is* that?" laughs the pop star judge, and I shrug modestly, like: *just some new shizzle*. We look at each other – we've never really put a name to it, and I reckon if I said the words "synchronized" and "swimming" in front of everyone Pete might push me out of the tank.

My hand slips off the edge of the pool and I put it back on again. But it slips off again and so does Gabe's. We glance at our hands, then at each other, but the judges are still talking so we try to focus on them. There's a ripple in the water, a strange *Jurassic Park*-style vibration that Roman and Pete don't seem to feel but Gabe and I do.

The surface of the water looks strange, and other people are beginning to notice it too. A couple of the stagehands walk briskly towards us and the audience falls silent, confused.

Whenever I remember this bit later, it's always in slow motion; maybe it was so unexpected that that's the only speed at which I could process it.

One side of this *massive* tank detaches and falls backwards, off the stage.

I watch it fall with a dreamy indifference and I'm vaguely aware of shouting. Someone grabs at my arms but they can't hang on to me. My legs are cold and everything feels suddenly hazy.

The four of us lurch downwards as the rest of the pool collapses and the water races towards the judges. Nothing feels like slow motion any more. Gabe and I clutch each other as the water throws us towards the judges' table and my head is submerged. Burning water shoots up my nose. I need to cough, I wrench my head upwards but there's just more water. Where *is* up? I can hear my heartbeat pounding in my ears, then people screaming, then heartbeat again, as my head is ducked in and out of water.

There's a sharp pain in my lower back as I hit something – the table, a camera, a *person...*? Gabriel's hand slips from mine; I grab fruitlessly at nothing but can't find him again and for the second time that month I lose consciousness.

36

I wake up to the rustle of crisp sheets and a strangely familiar pressure on my chest. You only get tucked in this hard at hospital.

It's a sign of an "interesting" life when you wake up in hospital so regularly that you can guess where you are with your eyes closed.

When I open them, Mum and Lav are sitting by the bed and Dad's in a chair in the corner – just like our last visit. But no one's crying this time.

They look delighted to see I'm awake and grin at me – the mood is definitely less serious. A nurse comes in to adjust my drip and check my charts. I think I recognize her from last time.

Ugh, except this time it feels like I'm wearing a polo neck made of cement. I'm in a neck brace and it's giving me an unfortunate double chin. I prop my jaw on the side, hoping that helps.

Lav gets to the point with characteristic gentleness.

"Now you're not dead, do you want the good news or the bad news?"

My throat hurts, so I hold up one finger, choosing option one.

"You nearly killed the judges of *BHT*."

I raise my eyebrows high.

"Well," she shrugs, "they're annoying; I think it's a fine achievement."

"The boys are OK," says Dad. "You got the worst of it."

I roll my eyes. Of course I did.

"Now get some rest," says Mum, putting a cool hand on my forehead. I turn my head to one side, trying to get comfortable, basking in the glow of our amazing performance. All that hard work, the nerves and the disasters, it was all worth it! We're TV stars.

I smile to myself, closing my eyes. I don't think I've ever been this happy. I'm a winner again – the Goldfish returns from the dead!

I have the unmistakable feeling I'm being watched. I open my eyes and Mum, Dad and Lav are all gathered tightly around my bed, looking down at me. Dad brushes my hair back from my face. Aaah, love my family.

I close my eyes again.

I open them again. Family still clustered around my bed.

OK, gang. It's been emotional, but give a girl some *space*. How am I meant to have a nap while you're all gazing at me like I've just been born? Although I suppose I should get used to this; famous people have to put up with it all the time.

Imagine how everyone at school is going to act around me now? Cammie's gonna be gutted! Maybe Melia will finally get the guts to talk to me? Can't promise I'll be too keen. After all, I've got friends now: proper friends.

Mum interrupts the little victory parade in my head.

"Lou, you were wonderful out there. It was a beautiful routine, wasn't it?" She turns to Dad and Lav.

"Amazing." Lav nods. "You're a choreographer!"

"Weirdest thing I've ever seen," admits Dad. "Don't know what goes on in that head of yours."

"We're all so proud of you." Mum smooths my hair behind my ear. "But you didn't get through to the next round."

I blink at her.

I think I must've gone temporarily insane. Because, and you'll laugh when I tell you, it's so ridiculous, but it *sounded* like she just said—

"You didn't go through. Debs' team did," adds Lav, clearly going for the "rip the plaster off quickly" approach.

"*What?*" I croak. My jaw slips off the side of the neck brace.

"Darling," says Mum, "they couldn't use the footage."

"They think the damage to the stage, crew and audience might run to six figures," Dad chips in.

"They might have to delay the next series because so many of the crew and judges are injured." Lav brings up the rear of the Bad News conga.

"I see. Anything else?"

"I got a parking ticket," Dad says. "Which I'm appealing, because the sign said..." He subsides at a look from Lav. "Nothing else, that's all."

"Try and get some sleep," says Mum, and they all tiptoe out of the room to leave me "in peace". AKA to stew in my rage.

I spend the next few days in hospital having X-rays to check I haven't chipped my spine or anything fun like that. But thankfully I'm not the unluckiest person in the world, I've just got bruises.

After a day or so, Gabe hobbles in to see me with a sprained ankle and a plaster on his throat. He has a proud smile on his face and presents me with the sign from our dressing room: LOU BROWN AND THE AQUARIUM BOYS.

"Did they give you that?" I ask, delighted.

"Not exactly…"

I turn the sign over and see large chips of paint on the back where he wrestled it off the door.

I examine the sign extremely carefully, suddenly a bit shy. Gabe sits on my bed, but my bedsheets are tucked in so tightly that him doing that pulls me towards him until I'm lying on my side. We're very close now, and when I look up his face is right next to mine. And all I can think is: *Beau Michaels tongue worms, Beau Michaels tongue worms.*

Lav! She's psychologically scarred me before I've had a chance to do any kissing of my own! But I'm only cross for a second because Gabe moves his face closer to mine and suddenly I *am* doing kissing of my own. Gabe's lips are soft and there is no darting tongue action at all. I feel smug. I'm clearly having better kissing than

Lav was. I smell the sweet hair product from the aquarium and realize that was Gabe, not Roman.

We're holding hands while we kiss but as he moves closer we break away, laughing. I don't know if you've ever tried to hug someone with a large cardboard sign between you, but it's difficult, risky work. We break apart, ruefully rubbing our chins where the sign poked us.

"When you get out of hospital, would you like to do something?" he asks.

"Do? Like a new swimming team?" I suggest. Just in case he doesn't mean a date; I don't want to embarrass myself.

"No, like a date!" he exclaims, rolling his eyes.

He did mean do something like a date!

"Cool, sure, whatev," I shrug. "I'm pretty chill about it, but if I have time, you know..."

Gabe gets up and props the sign on my windowsill where I can see it. "Go to sleep, you're very annoying," he says and kisses me on the cheek.

He leaves, but I don't go to sleep, I just lie there looking at my sign.

After a while I get a stiff neck so I turn my head towards the door. There's a little plastic bag sitting in the doorway like a visitor. I get up to investigate but Nurse Juliet notices and runs in, hissing, *"Bedrest!"* so I clamber back into bed. She hands me the bag, and when I root through it I find ten new pairs of pants. I did need new pants tbh, but not mysterious ones.

Hm. Either:

(1) I have a secret admirer who's weird but helpful,

(2) I've had a visit from the Pants Fairy, or

(3) they're magic and I've actually got a place at Hogwarts.

Gabe returns a few hours later with Pete (broken fingers), Roman (bruised ribs, cut legs) and Lav (absolutely fine). The boys aren't on bed rest, so they've been more active than me and have been picking up all the news that we missed after we destroyed *Britain's Hidden Talent*.

Pete is very excited. "So apparently, while there's no chance we'll make it on to the show because the studio cameras got water damage, loads of people filmed us on their phones and put the videos on YouTube, where the views have already overtaken our first video!"

Ro is adamant that this is way better than being on

the show because we get all the fame but also a kind of underground edgy vibe.

"Good, I'm glad," I say vaguely. "That's exactly the sort of vibe I've always wanted."

I'm distracted – Lav is sitting a little too close to Roman on my bed. I give her a narrow look.

Later, when the boys have gone, she pre-empts me: "But he's so lovely!"

"I know!" I say. "That's why you'd better be nice to him."

"He was so worried about you, he wouldn't get in the ambulance until he saw you were OK."

That is very sweet. And I'm happy for the two of them. I wonder if Ro does the tongue worm thing? I smirk to myself. It'd be funny if Lav got the bad kisser in the family and I got the good one. Rude to brag, though.

Lav hops off the bed to leave. "Did you get the bag of pants I left you?" she asks.

The smirk droops on my face. "Uh. Yes, thank you," I reply, smoothing my duvet and avoiding eye contact. "When did you leave it there, out of interest?"

Lav checks her watch. "I'm not sure. What time did you start snogging Gabe? I got here about a second before that."

I stare at the duvet feeling the blood rush to my ears.

"Thank you for stopping by, Lavender."

"Is he your boyfriend?"

"Please go, I'm very ill, I need my rest."

"This is adorable. *Gabe!!*"

I put my head under the pillow until my ears cool down.

EPILOGUE

I race towards an unfamiliar sports centre, taking the steps two at a time.

"Come *on*!" I yell over my shoulder. I run inside and look frantically around. Ah, that way! I look back and point. "This way, come on!"

Gabe staggers through the door after me, panting. "Yelling *come on* doesn't make my legs longer. If it did, I'd shout at them too."

I feel a stab of guilt and maybe love. (Or a stitch.) I grab his bag from him to lighten his load.

"I can carry you if you're tired."

"Shut up and keep moving."

We had to take three buses to get here, we've been rushing for about two hours and we're *still* late. The chlorine smell is getting stronger as we power-walk along the corridor, and I push through a set of heavy doors to find myself in the viewing gallery of a huge glass-roofed space with four swimming pools in it.

I flop down on a bench and start scanning the swimmers for a familiar face. A second later Gabe lands beside me with a thud. We both glow with sweaty heat. Gabe pulls off his jumper. I don't, not yet.

"I'm glad your dad's got a job," he grumbles, his jumper halfway over his head, "but I miss the free taxi service."

"The food's gone downhill too," I tell him. "Mum fried pasta leftovers the other day. Oh!" I spot her and pinch Gabe accidentally hard.

"Ow! Good!" He rubs his arm and we both wave.

Hannah is standing by the blocks getting ready for her race. I'm so glad we made it in time. I wave frantically to get her attention. The family behind me tut but I don't care. She spots me and gives me an aggressive thumbs-ups in return.

I unzip my hoodie to reveal my T-shirt.

It's bespoke. (Up yours, Debs.) It's got a giant photo of Hannah's sleeping face on it – I stand up and point at it.

She looks subtly delighted – although to the untrained

eye her expression could be mistaken for annoyed and embarrassed.

I settle down next to Gabe and we lean forward watching intently, no more joking around. Hannah's competing to get into the High Performance Training Camp again. I know she can make the times, and she'll deal better with the pressure this time. Especially since she had a Firm Word with her parents.

I see Debs talking to her. She's coaching her again. Hannah nods, listening. Debs' synchronized swimming team, Pretty in Sync, made the semi-finals of *Britain's Hidden Talent*. When they were eliminated before the finals, Debs stormed the stage and had to be dragged off the judges' table by security. She became briefly notorious.

I think public shame has been good for her. Character-building, or something. All I know is, I loved it. I watched that video *a lot* online. Along with thousands of other people.

Hannah gets up on her block. The room calms down. She is not looking at the other swimmers now but straight ahead. You swim no one's race but your own.

I hope she knows that if she hates the camp this time round, I'm still available for prison breaks.

She bends and wrap her fingers round the edge of the block. There's a pause, then the starting pistol bangs and she dives, hard.

I watch Hannah and Gabe watches me. I feel his eyes on me, and I smile and grab his hand. I'm swimming my own race.

ACKNOWLEDGEMENTS

Thanks, Mum and Dad! Top billing for long service.

Thanks to my tenacious and brilliant agent, Hellie Ogden at Janklow and Nesbit – for finding me in the aftermath of disaster and insisting that NOW was the perfect time to write this book. You were right, you're always right!

The original Lou – Lu Corfield, for letting me live and write in your house when I suddenly had nowhere to go. (This happens to me far too often. Must concentrate.)

My wonderful UK editor, Emma Lidbury at Walker, for her support, encouragement and – most importantly – great notes. Thanks for your patience with my chronology, somehow in Lou's world it's always Tuesday and then we lose a month. No one knows why.

Love and thanks to Walker Books, which is exactly

the sort of place you imagine that books get made. And where everyone is always welcoming even when I'm stealing books. Special thanks to Ed Ripley and the sales and marketing team; and, in the fiction team, Jack Noel, David McDougall, Jane Winterbotham, Gill Evans and Lucy Earley.

I'm very grateful to Jessica Fullalove, an awesome British swimmer who patiently answered all my divvy questions about her job.

I'm very excited to be published by Pan Macmillan in America, thank you so much Jean Feiwel for making that happen and Anna Roberto for ensuring that Lou makes sense when she travels! (The whole pants/pants thing was a minefield.)

Thank you to my European publishers – Gallimard Jeunesse in France, cbt Verlag in Germany and Piemme in Italy – I'm delighted that Lou is becoming more well-travelled than me! And to Rebecca Folland and Kirsty Gordon at Janklow and Nesbit for all their skill and patience. International tax is a world of pain that I won't ever understand – but hey, at least we TRIED? (If HMRC is reading this … I swear, I paid.)

Nat

Margot/Stinkbox

Girl Out of Water is Nat's first book for teens, and she says Lou is a less mopey, spotty, migrainey version of her as a teenager. Nat lives in South London with her kitten, Margot/Stinkbox. By the time you read this she might be a cat.

Nat was a stand-up comedian and sketch performer for seven years, which means she went to bed late and had crisps for dinner for ALMOST A DECADE. She is now a BAFTA-nominated screenwriter, director, actor and author. Her first book, *Cuckoo in the Nest*, is a comic memoir for adults that was a *Sunday Times* Book of the Year.

If you are interested in what Nat is thinking RIGHT NOW, check out @natluurtsema.

#girloutofwater   www.girloutofwater.com

An inspirational and heart-warming story that celebrates
friendship and finding your place in the world.

Amber, Maali, Sky and Rose may be very
different, but they all have one thing in
common: they're fed up with being told
how to look, what to think and how to act.

They're not like everyone else
and they don't want to be.

*Becoming friends gives them
the courage to be themselves.*